PENGUI

THE RELUCTAN

Mohsin Hamid writes regularly for *The New York Times*, the *Guardian* and the *New York Review of Books*, and is the author of *The Reluctant Fundamentalist*, *Moth Smoke*, *How to Get Filthy Rich in Rising Asia*, *Discontent and its Civilizations* and *Exit West*. Born and raised mostly in Lahore, he has since lived between Lahore, London and New York.

George Morton-Clark is an international painter who describes his work as 'the world as a colliding of consciousness'. He is represented by Saatchi Gallery and is regularly exhibited around the world. His work focuses on people, and perceptions of reality, either emotional or cultural. He lives in London.

The Reluctant Fundamentalist

MOHSIN HAMID

PENGUIN BOOKS

PENGUIN ESSENTIALS

UK | USA | Canada | Ireland | Australia
India | New Zealand | South Africa

Penguin Books is part of the Penguin Random House group of companies
whose addresses can be found at global.penguinrandomhouse.com.

First published in Great Britain by Hamish Hamilton 2007
Published in Penguin Books 2007
This Penguin Essentials edition published 2017
004

Portions of this novel were previously published
in somewhat different form in the *Paris Review*

Printed in Great Britain by Clays Ltd, Elcograf S.p.A.

A CIP catalogue record for this book is available from the British Library

ISBN: 978-0-241-98138-2

www.greenpenguin.co.uk

The Reluctant Fundamentalist

I

Excuse me, sir, but may I be of assistance? Ah, I see I have alarmed you. Do not be frightened by my beard: I am a lover of America. I noticed that you were looking for something; more than looking, in fact you seemed to be on a *mission,* and since I am both a native of this city and a speaker of your language, I thought I might offer you my services.

How did I know you were American? No, not by the color of your skin; we have a range of complexions in this country, and yours occurs often among the people of our northwest frontier. Nor was it your dress that gave you away; a European tourist could as easily have purchased in Des Moines your suit, with its single vent, and your button-down shirt. True, your hair, short-cropped, and your expansive chest—the chest, I would say, of a man who bench-presses regularly, and maxes out well above two-twenty-five—are typical of a certain *type* of American; but then again, sportsmen and soldiers of all nationalities tend to look alike. Instead, it was your *bearing* that allowed me to identify you, and I do not mean that as an insult, for I see your face has hardened, but merely as an observation.

Come, tell me, what were you looking for? Surely, at this time of day, only one thing could have brought you to the district of Old Anarkali—named, as you may be aware, after a courtesan immured for loving a prince—and that is the quest for the perfect cup of tea. Have I guessed correctly? Then allow me, sir, to suggest my favorite among these many establishments. Yes, this is the one. Its metal chairs are no better upholstered, its wooden tables are equally rough, and it is, like the others, open to the sky. But the quality of its tea, I assure you, is unparalleled.

You prefer that seat, with your back so close to the wall? Very well, although you will benefit less from the intermittent breeze, which, when it does blow, makes these warm afternoons more pleasant. And will you not remove your jacket? So formal!

Now *that* is not typical of Americans, at least not in my experience. And my experience is substantial: I spent four and a half years in your country. Where? I worked in New York, and before that attended college in New Jersey. Yes, you are right: it *was* Princeton! Quite a guess, I must say.

What did I think of Princeton? Well, the answer to that question requires a story. When I first arrived, I looked around me at the Gothic buildings—younger, I later learned, than many of the mosques of this city, but made through acid treatment and ingenious stonemasonry to look older—and thought, *This is a dream come true*. Princeton inspired in me the feeling that my life was a film in which I was the star and everything was possible. *I have access to this beautiful campus,* I thought, *to professors who are titans in their fields and fellow students who are philosopher-kings in the making.*

I was, I must admit, overly generous in my initial assumptions about the standard of the student body. They were almost all intelligent, and many were brilliant, but whereas I was one of only two Pakistanis in my entering class—two from a population of over a hundred million souls, mind you—

the Americans faced much less daunting odds in the selection process. A thousand of your compatriots were enrolled, five hundred times as many, even though your country's population was only twice that of mine. As a result, the non-Americans among us tended on average to do better than the Americans, and in my case I reached my senior year without having received a single B.

Looking back now, I see the power of that system, pragmatic and effective, like so much else in America. We international students were sourced from around the globe, sifted not only by well-honed standardized tests but by painstakingly customized evaluations—interviews, essays, recommendations—until the best and the brightest of us had been identified. I myself had among the top exam results in Pakistan and was besides a soccer player good enough to compete on the varsity team, which I did until I damaged my knee in my sophomore year. Students like me were given visas and scholarships, complete financial aid, mind you, and invited into the ranks of the meritocracy. In return, we were expected to contribute our talents to your society, the society we were joining.

And for the most part, we were happy to do so. I certainly was, at least at first.

Every fall, Princeton raised her skirt for the corporate recruiters who came onto campus and—as you say in America—showed them some skin. The skin Princeton showed was good skin, of course—young, eloquent, and clever as can be—but even among all that skin, I knew in my senior year that I was something special. I was a perfect breast, if you will—tan, succulent, seemingly defiant of gravity—and I was confident of getting any job I wanted.

Except one: Underwood Samson & Company. You have not heard of them? They were a valuation firm. They told their clients how much businesses were worth, and they did so, it was said, with a precision that was uncanny. They were small—a boutique, really, employing a bare minimum of people—and they paid well, offering the fresh graduate a base salary of over eighty thousand dollars. But more importantly, they gave one a robust set of skills and an exalted brand name, so exalted, in fact, that after two or three years there as an analyst, one was virtually guaranteed admission to Harvard Business School. Because of this, over a hundred members of the Princeton Class of 2001 sent their grades and résumés to Underwood Samson. Eight were selected—not for jobs, I should make clear, but for interviews—and one of them was me.

You seem worried. Do not be; this burly fellow is merely our waiter, and there is no need to reach under your jacket, I assume to grasp your wallet, as we will pay him later, when we are done. Would you prefer regular tea, with milk and sugar, or green tea, or perhaps their more fragrant specialty, Kashmiri tea? Excellent choice. I will have the same, and perhaps a plate of jalebis as well. There. He has gone. I must admit, he is a rather intimidating chap. But irreproachably polite: you would have been surprised by the sweetness of his speech, if only you understood Urdu.

Where were we? Ah yes, Underwood Samson. On the day of my interview, I was uncharacteristically nervous. They had sent a single interviewer, and he received us in a room at the Nassau Inn, an ordinary room, mind you, not a suite; they knew we were sufficiently impressed already. When my turn came, I entered and found a man physically not unlike yourself; he, too, had the look of a seasoned army officer. "Changez?" he said, and I nodded, for that is indeed my name. "Come on in and take a seat."

His name was Jim, he told me, and I had precisely fifty minutes to convince him to offer me a job. "Sell yourself," he said. "What makes you special?" I began with my transcript, pointing out that I was on track to graduate *summa cum laude,* that I had, as I have mentioned, yet to receive a single B. "I'm sure you're smart," he said, "but none of the people I'm talking to today has any Bs." This, for me, was an unsettling revelation. I told him that I was tenacious, that after injuring my knee I had made it through physiotherapy in half the time the doctors expected, and while I could no longer play varsity soccer, I could once again run a mile in less than six minutes. "That's good," he said, and for the first time it seemed to me I had made something of an impression on him, when he added, "but what else?"

I fell silent. I am, as you can see, normally quite happy to chat, but in that moment I did not know what to say. I watched him watch me, trying to understand what he was looking for. He glanced down at my résumé, which was lying between us on the table, and then back up again. His eyes were cold, a pale blue, and *judgmental,* not in the way that word is normally used, but in the sense of being professionally appraising, like a jeweler's when he inspects out of curiosity a diamond he intends neither to buy nor to sell. Finally, after some time had passed—it could not have been more than a minute, but it felt longer—he said, "Tell me something. Where are you from?"

I said I was from Lahore, the second largest city of Pakistan, ancient capital of the Punjab, home to nearly as many people as New York, layered like a sedimentary plain with the accreted history of invaders from the Aryans to the Mongols to the British. He merely nodded. Then he said, "And are you on financial aid?"

I did not answer him at once. I knew there were subjects interviewers were not permitted to broach—religion, for example, and sexual orientation—and I suspected financial aid was one of these. But that was not why I hesitated; I hesitated because his question made me feel uncomfortable. Then I said, "Yes." "And isn't it harder," he asked, "for international students to get in if they apply for aid?" Again I said, "Yes." "So," he said, "you must have really needed the money." And for the third time, I said, "Yes."

Jim leaned back in his chair and crossed his legs at the knee, just as you are doing now. Then he said, "You're polished, well-dressed. You have this sophisticated accent. Most people probably assume you're rich where you come from." It was not a question, so I made no reply. "Do your friends here know," he went on, "that your family couldn't afford to send you to Princeton without a scholarship?"

This was, as I have said, the most important of my interviews, and I knew moreover that I ought to remain calm, but I was getting annoyed, and I had had enough of this line of questioning. So I said, "Excuse me, Jim, but is there a point to all this?" It came out more aggressively than I intended, my voice rising and taking on an edge. "So they don't know," Jim said. He smiled and went on, "You have a temper. I like that. I went to Princeton, too. Class of '81. *Summa cum laude.*" He winked. "I was the first guy from my family to go to college. I worked a night shift in Trenton to pay my way, far enough from campus that people wouldn't find out. So I get where you're coming from, Changez. You're hungry, and that's a good thing in my book."

I was, I must confess, caught off balance. I did not know how to react. But I did know that I was impressed with Jim; he had, after all, seen through me in a few minutes more clearly than had many people who had known me for years. I could understand why he would be effective at valuations, and why—by extension—his firm had come to be highly regarded in this field. I was also pleased that he had found in me something he prized, and my confidence, until now shaken by our encounter, began to recover.

It is worth, if you will permit me, my indulging in a minor digression at this point. I am not poor; far from it: my great-grandfather, for example, was a barrister with the means to endow a school for the Muslims of the Punjab. Like him, my grandfather and father both attended university in England. Our family home sits on an acre of land in the middle of

Gulberg, one of the most expensive districts of this city. We employ several servants, including a driver and a gardener—which would, in America, imply that we were a family of great wealth.

But we are not rich. The men and women—yes, the women, too—of my household are working people, professionals. And the half-century since my great-grandfather's death has not been a prosperous one for professionals in Pakistan. Salaries have not risen in line with inflation, the rupee has declined steadily against the dollar, and those of us who once had substantial family estates have seen them divided and subdivided by each—larger—subsequent generation. So my grandfather could not afford what his father could, and my father could not afford what *his* father could, and when the time came to send me to college, the money simply was not there.

But status, as in any traditional, class-conscious society, declines more slowly than wealth. So we retain our Punjab Club membership. We continue to be invited to the functions and weddings and parties of the city's elite. And we look with a mixture of disdain and envy upon the rising class of entrepreneurs—owners of businesses legal and

illegal—who power through the streets in their
BMW SUVs. Our situation is, perhaps, not so
different from that of the old European aristocracy
in the nineteenth century, confronted by the
ascendance of the bourgeoisie. Except, of course,
that we are part of a broader malaise afflicting not
only the formerly rich but much of the formerly
middle-class as well: a growing inability to purchase
what we previously could.

Confronted with this reality, one has two choices:
pretend all is well or work hard to restore things
to what they were. I chose both. At Princeton, I
conducted myself in public like a young prince,
generous and carefree. But I also, as quietly as I
could, held down three on-campus jobs—in infre-
quently visited locations, such as the library of the
Program in Near Eastern Studies—and prepared
for my classes throughout the night. Most people
I met were taken in by my public persona. Jim was
not. But fortunately, where I saw shame, he saw
opportunity. And he was, in some ways but not in
all—as I would later come to understand—correct.

Ah, our tea has arrived! Do not look so sus-
picious. I assure you, sir, nothing untoward will

happen to you, not even a runny stomach. After all, it is not as if it has been *poisoned*. Come, if it makes you more comfortable, let me switch my cup with yours. Just so. How much sugar would you like? None? Very unusual, but I will not insist. Do try these sticky, orange sweets—jalebis—but be careful, they are hot! I see you approve. Yes, they are delicious. It is curious how a cup of tea can be refreshing even on a warm day such as this—a mystery, really—but there you have it.

I was telling you about my interview with Underwood Samson, and how Jim had found me to be, as he put it, *hungry*. I waited to see what he would say next, and what he said next was this: "All right, Changez, let's test you out. I'm going to give you a business case, a company I want you to value. You can ask me anything you need to know—think Twenty Questions—and you can do your calculations with that pencil and paper. Ready?" I said that I was, and he continued: "I'm going to throw you a curve ball. You're going to need to get creative here. The company is simple. It has only one service line: instantaneous travel. You step into its terminal in New York, and you immediately reappear in its terminal in London. Like a transporter on *Star Trek*. Get it? Good. Let's go."

I would like to think that I was, in that moment, outwardly calm, but inside I was panicking. How does one value a fictitious, fantastic company such as the one he had just described? Where does one even begin? I had no idea. I looked at Jim, but he did not seem to be joking. So I inhaled and shut my eyes. There was a mental state I used to attain when I was playing soccer: my self would disappear, and I would be free, free of doubts and limits, free to focus on nothing but the game. When I entered this state I felt unstoppable. Sufi mystics and Zen masters would, I suspect, understand the feeling. Possibly, ancient warriors did something similar before they went into battle, ritualistically accepting their impending death so they could function unencumbered by fear.

I entered this state in the interview. My essence was focused on finding my way through the case. I started by asking questions to understand the technology: how scalable it was, how reliable, how safe. Then I asked Jim about the environment: if there were any direct competitors, what the

regulators might do, if any suppliers were particularly critical. Then I went into the cost side to
figure out what expenses we would have to cover.
And last I looked at revenues, using the Concorde
for comparison, as an example of the price premium
and demand one gets for cutting travel time in half,
and then estimating how much more one would
get for cutting it to zero. Once I had done all that, I
projected profits out into the future and discounted
them to net present value. And in the end, I arrived
at a number.

"Two point three billion dollars," I said. Jim was
silent for a while. Then he shook his head. "Wildly
overoptimistic," he said. "Your assumptions on
customers adopting this thing are way too high.
Would you be willing to step into a machine, be
dematerialized, and then recomposed thousands of
miles away? This is exactly the kind of hyped-up
bullshit our clients pay Underwood Samson to see
through." I hung my head. "But," Jim continued,
"your approach was right on. You have what it
takes. All you need is training and experience." He
extended his hand. "You've got an offer. We'll give
you one week to decide."

At first I did not believe him. I asked if he was serious, if there was not a second round for me to pass. "We're a small firm," he said. "We don't waste time. Besides, I'm in charge of analyst recruiting. I don't need another opinion." I noticed his hand was still hanging in the air between us, and—fearful it might be withdrawn—I reached out and shook it. His grip was firm and seemed to communicate to me, in that moment, that Underwood Samson had the potential to transform my life as surely as it had transformed his, making my concerns about money and status things of the distant past.

I walked back to my dormitory—Edwards Hall, it was called—later that same afternoon. The sky was a brilliant blue, so different from the orange, dusty sky above us today, and I felt something well up inside me, a sense of pride so strong that it made me lift my head and yell, as much to my own surprise as I am sure it was to the other students passing by: "Thank you, God!"

Yes, it was exhilarating. *That,* in an admittedly long-winded fashion, is how I think, looking back, about Princeton. Princeton made everything possible for me. But it did not, *could* not, make me forget such things as how much I enjoy the tea in this, the city of my birth, steeped long enough to acquire a rich, dark color, and made creamy with fresh, full-fat milk. It is excellent, no? I see you have finished yours. Allow me to pour you another cup.

2

Do you see those girls, walking there, in jeans speckled with paint? Yes, they *are* attractive. And how different they look from the women of that family sitting at the table beside ours, in their traditional dress. The National College of Arts is not far—it is, as a matter of fact, only around the corner—and its students often come here for a cup of tea, just as we are doing now. I see one in particular has caught your eye; she is indeed a beauty. Tell me, sir, have you left behind a love—male or female, I do not presume to know your preference, although the intensity of your gaze suggests the latter—in your homeland?

Your shrug is inscrutable, but I will be more forthcoming. I did leave behind a love, and her name was Erica. We met the summer after we graduated, part of a group of Princetonians who had decided to holiday together in Greece. She and the others were members of the university's most prestigious eating club, Ivy, and were traveling courtesy of gifts from their parents or dividends from their trust funds, which they were now of an age to access; I had cooked my own meals in the basement kitchen of my dormitory and was there thanks to my sign-on bonus from Underwood Samson. I was friendly with one of the Ivy men, Chuck, from my days on the soccer team, and was well-liked as an exotic acquaintance by some of the others, whom I had met through him.

We assembled in Athens, having arrived on different flights, and when I first saw Erica, I could not prevent myself from offering to carry her backpack—so stunningly *regal* was she. Her hair was piled up like a tiara on her head, and her navel—ah, what a navel: made firm, I would later learn, by years of tae kwon do—was visible beneath a short T-shirt bearing an image of Chairman Mao. We were introduced, she smiled as she shook my hand—whether because she found me irresistibly refined or oddly anachronistic, I did not know— and then we headed off with the group to the port city of Piraeus.

It was immediately apparent that I would not have, in my wooing of Erica, the field to myself. In fact, no sooner had we set sail on our ferry to the islands than did a young man—a tooth dangling on a string of leather in front of his bare, but meagerly muscled, chest—begin to strum his guitar and serenade her from across the deck. "What language is that?" she asked me, leaning close enough for her breath to tickle my ear. "English, I believe," I replied after much concentration. "As a matter of fact, it is Bryan Adams, 'Summer of '69'." She laughed. "You're right," she said, politely lowering her voice to add, "Wow, he's terrible!" I was inclined to agree, but now that I knew the troubadour posed no threat, I chose to maintain a magnanimous silence instead.

A more serious challenge would come from Chuck's good—and similarly monosyllabically monikered—friend Mike, who, the next day, as we sat in a restaurant overhanging the lip of the shattered volcano that is the island of Santorini, casually extended his arm along the back of Erica's chair and remained in that position, which surely became uncomfortable, for the better part of an hour. Erica made no sign that she wished him to remove his arm, but I drew some consolation from the fact that throughout the dinner she listened *intently* when I spoke, smiling from time to time and training her green eyes upon me. Afterwards, however, on the walk to our pension, she and Mike trailed behind the rest of us, and that night I found it difficult to sleep.

In the morning, I was relieved to see that she came down to breakfast *before* Mike—not with him—and I was also pleased that we appeared to be the first two of our group to be awake. She spread jam on a croissant, gave half to me, and said, "You know what I'd like to do?" I asked her what. "I'd like to stay here by myself," she said, "rent a room on one of these islands and just write." I told her she should, but she shook her head. "I wouldn't last a week," she said. "I'm not good at being alone. But you, on the other hand," and here she tilted her head and crossed her arms, "I think you'd be fine."

I have never, to the best of my knowledge, had any fear of solitude, and so I shrugged in assent and said, by way of explanation, "When I was a child, there were eight of us, eight cousins, all in the same compound—a single boundary wall surrounded the plot of land my grandfather left to his sons, you see—and we had between us as many as three dogs and, for a time, a duck." She laughed, and then she said, "So being alone was a luxury, huh?" I nodded. "You give off this strong sense of home," she said. "You know that? This I'm-from-a-big-family vibe. It's nice. It makes you feel solid." I was pleased— even though I was not sure I fully understood—and said thank you for want of anything better to say. Then, hesitantly because I did not wish to be too forward, I asked, "And you, do you feel solid?"

She considered this and said, with what I thought was a trace of sadness in her voice, "Sometimes, but no, not really." Before I could respond we were joined by Chuck, and then by Mike, and the conversation turned to beaches and hangovers and the timings of ferries. But when I looked at Erica and she looked back at me, I felt we both under-stood that something had been exchanged between us, the first invitation to a friendship, perhaps, and so I waited patiently for an opportunity to resume our discussion.

Such an opportunity would not come for quite

some time—not until several days later, as a matter of fact. You might imagine I grew frustrated with the wait, but you must remember: I had never in my life had a vacation like this one. We rented motor scooters and purchased straw mats to spread on beaches of black volcanic sand, which the sun had made too hot for bare skin; we stayed in the rooms of quaint houses let out in the summertime by elderly couples to tourists; we ate grilled octopus and drank sparkling water and red wine. I had not before this been to Europe or even swum in the sea—Lahore is, as you know, a ninety-minute journey by air from the coast—and so I gave in to the pleasures of being among this wealthy young fellowship.

I will admit that there were *details* which annoyed me. The ease with which they parted with money, for example, thinking nothing of the occasional— but not altogether infrequent—meal costing perhaps fifty dollars a head. Or their self-righteousness in dealing with those whom they had paid for a service. "But you *told* us," they would say to Greeks twice their age, before insisting things be done their way. I, with my finite and depleting reserve of cash and my traditional sense of deference to one's seniors, found myself wondering by what quirk of human history my companions—many of whom I would have regarded as upstarts in my own country, so devoid of refinement were they—were in a position to conduct themselves in the world as though they were its ruling class.

But it may be that I am inclined to exaggerate these irritants in retrospect, knowing the course my relationship with your country would later take. Besides, the rest of the group was for me mere background; in the foreground shimmered Erica, and observing her gave me enormous satisfaction. She had told me that she hated to be alone, and I came to notice that she rarely was. She attracted people to her; she had presence, an uncommon *magnetism*. Documenting her effect on her habitat, a naturalist would likely have compared her to a lioness: strong, sleek, and invariably surrounded by her pride.

Yet one got the sense that she existed internally at a degree of remove from those around her. Not that she was aloof; she was, in fact, friendly in disposition. But one felt that some part of her—and this, perhaps, was a not insubstantial component of her appeal—was out of reach, lost in thoughts unsaid. Suffice it to say that in relationship to the contemporary female icons of your country, she belonged more to the camp of Paltrow than to that of Spears.

But my cultural reference has fallen on deaf ears! You appear distracted, sir; those pretty girls from the National College of Arts have clearly recaptured your attention. Or are you watching that man, the one with the beard far longer than mine, who has stopped to stand beside them? You think he will scold them for the inappropriateness of their dress— their T-shirts and jeans? I suspect not: those girls seem comfortable in this area and are likely to come here often, while he looks out of place. Moreover, among the many rules that govern the bazaars of Lahore is this: if a woman is harassed by a man, she has the right to appeal to the brotherly instincts of the mob, and the mob is known to beat men who annoy their sisters. *There,* sir, you see? He has moved on. He was merely staring at something he found intriguing, much as you are, but in your case, of course, with considerably more discretion.

As for myself, that summer in Greece with Erica, I tried not to stare. But towards the end of our holiday, on the island of Rhodes, I could not help myself. You have not been to Rhodes? You must go. It seemed to me unlike the other islands we had visited. Its cities were fortified, protected by ancient castles; they guarded against the Turks, much like the army and navy and air force of modern Greece, part of a wall against the East that still stands. How strange it was for me to think I grew up on the other side!

But that is neither here nor there. I was telling you about the moment when I was forced to stare. We were lying on the beach, and many of the European women nearby were, as usual, sunbathing topless—a practice I wholeheartedly supported, but which the women among us Princetonians, unfortunately, had thus far failed to embrace—when I noticed Erica was untying the straps of her bikini. And then, as I watched, only an arm's length away, she bared her breasts to the sun.

A moment later—no, you are right: I am being dishonest; it was *more* than a moment—she turned her head to the side and saw me staring at her.

A number of possible alternatives presented themselves: I could suddenly avert my eyes, thereby proving not only that I had been staring but that I was uncomfortable with her nudity; I could, after a brief pause, casually move my gaze away, as though the sight of her breasts had been the most natural thing in the world; I could keep staring, honestly communicating in this way my admiration for what she had revealed; or I could, through well-timed literary allusion, draw her attention to the fact that there was a passage in *Mr. Palomar* that captured perfectly my dilemma.

But I did none of these things. Instead, I blushed and said, "Hello." She smiled—with uncharacteristic shyness, it seemed to me—and replied, "Hi." I nodded, tried to think of something else to say, failed, and said, "Hello," again. As soon as I had done this, I wanted to disappear; I knew I sounded unbelievably foolish. She started to laugh, her small breasts bouncing, and said, "I'm going for a swim." But then, as she walked away, she half-turned and added, "You want to come?"

I followed her, watching the muscles of her lower back tense delicately to stabilize her spine. We reached the water; it was warm and perfectly clear, round pebbles and the flash of little fish visible below the surface. We slipped inside, she swam out into the bay with powerful strokes, and then she trod water until I had caught up with her. For a time we were both silent and I felt our slippery legs graze each other as we churned the sea. "I don't think," she said finally, "I've ever met someone our age as polite as you." "Polite?" I said, less than radiant with joy. She smiled. "I don't mean it that way," she said. "Not *boring* polite. Respectful polite. You give people their space. I really like that. It's unusual."

We continued bobbing face to face, and I formed the impression that she was waiting for me to say something in reply, but words had abandoned me. Instead, my thoughts were engaged in a struggle to maintain a facial expression that would not appear idiotic. She turned and began to swim back to shore, keeping her head above water. I pulled alongside and—claiming victory at last over my cowering tongue—said, "Shall we return to town for a drink?" To which she replied, with a raised eyebrow and in an accent not normally her own, "I would be delighted to do so, sir."

On the beach she put on a shirt—a gentleman's shirt, I still remember, blue and fraying at the tips of the collar—and stuffed her towel and bikini top into a bag. None of our companions wanted to join us, there being at least another hour of tan-inducing sunlight remaining in the day, and so we two made our way to the road and caught a bus. As we sat side by side, I could not help but notice that her bare leg was less than an inch from where I was resting my hand on my thigh.

It is remarkable, I must say, how being in Pakistan heightens one's sensitivity to the sight of a woman's body. Do you not agree? That bearded man—who even now, sir, continues from time to time to attract your wary gaze—is himself unable to stop glancing over his shoulder at those girls, fifty yards away from him. Yet they are exposing only the flesh of the neck, the face, and the lower three-quarters of the arm! It is the effect of scarcity; one's rules of propriety make one *thirst* for the improper. Moreover, once sensitized in this manner, one numbs only slowly, if at all; I had by the summer of my trip to Greece spent four years in America already—and had experienced all the intimacies college students commonly experience—but still I remained acutely aware of visible female skin.

It was in order to prevent myself from impolitely focusing on Erica's wheat-colored limbs that I asked her if her shirt had belonged to her father. "No," she said, rubbing the fabric between her thumb and forefinger, "it was my boyfriend's." "Ah," I said, "I did not know you had a boyfriend." "He died last year," she said. "His name was Chris." I said I was sorry and told her that it was a fine shirt; Chris had had excellent taste. She agreed, saying that he had been quite the dandy, and rather vain even in hospital. His nurses had been charmed by him: he was a good-looking boy with what she described as an *Old World* appeal.

Arriving in town, we found a café near the harbor with tables shaded by blue-and-white umbrellas. She ordered a beer; I did the same. "So what's Pakistan like?" she asked. I told her Pakistan was many things, from seaside to desert to farmland stretched between rivers and canals; I told her that

I had driven with my parents and my brother to China on the Karakoram Highway, passing along the bottoms of valleys higher than the tops of the Alps; I told her that alcohol was illegal for Muslims to buy and so I had a Christian bootlegger who delivered booze to my house in a Suzuki pickup. She listened to me speak with a series of smiles, as though she were sipping at my descriptions and finding them to her taste. Then she said, "You miss home."

I shrugged. I often did miss home, but in that moment I was content to be where I was. She took out her notebook—it was bound with soft, orange leather; I had previously seen her scribbling in it during moments of repose—and passing it to me with a pencil said, "What does your writing look like?" I said, "Urdu is similar to Arabic, but we have more letters." She said, "Show me," and so I did. "It's beautiful," she said, meeting my eyes. "What's it mean?" "This is your name," I replied, "and this, underneath, is mine."

We stayed at our table, talking as the sun set, and she told me about Chris. They had grown up together—in facing apartments, children the same age with no siblings—and were best friends well before their first kiss, which happened when they were six but was not repeated until they were fifteen. He had a collection of European comic books with which they were obsessed, and they used to spend hours at home reading them and making their own: Chris drawing, Erica writing. They were both admitted to Princeton, but he had not come because he was diagnosed with lung cancer—he had had *one* cigarette, she said with a smile, but only the day after he received the results of his biopsy—and she had made sure she never had classes on a Friday so she could spend three days a week in New York with him. He died three years later, at the end of the spring semester of her junior year. "So I kind of miss home, too," she said. "Except my home was a guy with long, skinny fingers."

Later that evening, when we went out for dinner with the group, Erica chose the seat opposite mine. Chuck made all of us laugh with a series of uncanny impersonations—my mannerisms were, in my opinion, somewhat exaggerated, but the others were spot on—and then he went around the table and asked each of us to reveal our dream for what we would most like to be. When my turn came, I said I hoped one day to be the dictator of an Islamic republic with nuclear capability; the others appeared shocked, and I was forced to explain that I had been joking. Erica alone smiled; she seemed to understand my sense of humor.

Erica said that she wanted to be a novelist. Her creative thesis had been a work of long fiction that had won an award at Princeton; she intended to revise it for submission to literary agents and would see how they responded. Normally, Erica spoke little of herself, and tonight, when she did so, it was in a slightly lowered voice and with her eyes often on me. I felt—despite the presence of our companions, whose attention, as always, she managed to capture—that she was sharing with me an intimacy, and this feeling grew stronger when, after observing me struggle, she helped me separate the flesh from the bones of my fish without my having to ask.

Nothing physical happened between Erica and me in Greece; we did not so much as hold hands. But she gave me her number in New York, to which we were both returning, and she offered to help me settle in. For my part, I was content: I had struck up an acquaintance with a woman with whom I was well and truly smitten, and my excitement about the adventures my new life held for me had never been more pronounced.

But what is that? Ah, your mobile phone! I have not previously seen its like; it is, I suspect, one of those models capable of communicating via satellite when no ground coverage is available. Will you not answer it? I assure you, sir, I will do my *utmost* to avoid eavesdropping on your conversation. But you are opting to write a text message instead; very wise: often a few words are more than sufficient. As for myself, I am quite happy to wait as you navigate the keys. After all, those girls from the National College of Arts have only just finished their tea, and the pleasure of their presence on this street will persist for a few moments longer before they disappear—as inevitably they must—from view around that corner.

3

We locals treasure these last days of what passes for spring here in Lahore; the sun, although hot, has such a soothing effect. Or, I should say, it has such a soothing effect on *us,* for you, sir, continue to appear ill at ease. I hope you will not mind my saying so, but the frequency and purposefulness with which you glance about—a steady tick-tick-tick seeming to beat in your head as you move your gaze from one point to the next—brings to mind the behavior of an animal that has ventured too far from its lair and is now, in unfamiliar surroundings, uncertain whether it is predator or prey!

Come, relinquish your foreigner's sense of being watched. Observe instead how the shadows have lengthened. Soon they will shut to traffic the gates at either end of this market, transforming Old Anarkali into a pedestrian-only piazza. In fact, they have begun. Will the police arrest those boys on their motor scooter? Only if they can catch them! And already they are streaking away, making good their escape. But they will be the last to do so. The gates are now being locked, as you can see, and those gaps that remain are too narrow for anything wider than a man.

You will have noticed that the newer districts of Lahore are poorly suited to the needs of those who must walk. In their spaciousness—with their public parks and wide, tree-lined boulevards—they enforce an ancient hierarchy that comes to us from the countryside: the superiority of the mounted man over the man on foot. But here, where we sit, and in the even older districts that lie between us and the River Ravi—the congested, maze-like heart of this city—Lahore is more democratically *urban*. Indeed, in these places it is the man with four wheels who is forced to dismount and become part of the crowd.

Like Manhattan? Yes, precisely! And that was one of the reasons why for me moving to New York felt—so unexpectedly—like coming home. But there were other reasons as well: the fact that Urdu was spoken by taxicab drivers; the presence, only two blocks from my East Village apartment, of a

samosa- and channa-serving establishment called
the Pak-Punjab Deli; the coincidence of crossing
Fifth Avenue during a parade and hearing, from
loudspeakers mounted on the South Asian Gay and
Lesbian Association float, a song to which I had
danced at my cousin's wedding.

In a subway car, my skin would typically fall in
the middle of the color spectrum. On street corners,
tourists would ask me for directions. I was, in four
and a half years, never an American; I was *immediately* a New Yorker. What? My voice is rising? You
are right; I tend to become sentimental when I think
of that city. It still occupies a place of great fondness
in my heart, which is quite something, I must say,
given the circumstances under which, after only
eight months of residence, I would later depart.

Certainly, much of my early excitement about
New York was wrapped up in my excitement
about Underwood Samson. I remember my sense of
wonder on the day I reported for duty. Their offices
were perched on the forty-first and forty-second
floors of a building in midtown—higher than
any two structures here in Lahore would be if they
were stacked one atop the other—and while I had

previously flown in airplanes and visited the Himalayas, nothing had prepared me for the drama, the *power* of the view from their lobby. This, I realized, was another world from Pakistan; supporting my feet were the achievements of the most technologically advanced civilization our species had ever known.

Often, during my stay in your country, such comparisons troubled me. In fact, they did more than trouble me: they made me resentful. Four thousand years ago, we, the people of the Indus River basin, had cities that were laid out on grids and boasted underground sewers, while the ancestors of those who would invade and colonize America were illiterate barbarians. Now our cities were largely unplanned, unsanitary affairs, and America had universities with individual endowments greater than our national budget for education. To be reminded of this vast disparity was, for me, to be ashamed.

But not on that day. On that day, I did not think of myself as a Pakistani, but as an Underwood Samson trainee, and my firm's impressive offices made me *proud*. I wished I could show my parents

and my brother! I stood still, taking in the vista, but
not for long; soon after our arrival we entering
analysts were marched into a conference room for
our orientation presentation. There a vice president
by the name of Sherman—his head gleaming from
a recent shave—laid out the ethos of our new outfit.

"We're a meritocracy," he said. "We believe
in being the best. You were the best candidates at
the best schools in the country. That's what got you
here. But meritocracy doesn't stop with recruiting.
We'll rank you every six months. You'll know your
rankings. Your bonuses and staffing will depend
on them. If you do well, you'll be rewarded. If
you don't, you'll be out the door. It's that simple.
You'll have your first rankings at the end of this
training program."

Simple indeed. I glanced about me to see how
my fellow trainees were responding. There were
five of them, in addition to myself, and four sat
rigidly at attention; the fifth, a chap called Wainwright, was more relaxed. Twirling his pen between
his fingers in a fashion reminiscent of Val Kilmer in
Top Gun, he leaned towards me and whispered,
"No points for second place, Maverick." "You're

dangerous, Ice Man," I replied—attempting to approximate a naval aviator's drawl—and the two of us exchanged a grin.

But aside from light-hearted banter of this kind, there would be little in the way of fun and games at the workplace. For the next four weeks, our days followed a consistent routine. In the mornings we had a three-hour seminar: one of a series of modules that attempted to abridge an entire year of business school. We were taught by professors from the most prestigious institutions—a Wharton woman, for example, instructed us in finance—and the results of the tests we were administered were carefully recorded.

Lunch was taken in the cafeteria; over chicken-pesto-in-sun-dried-tomato wraps we observed the assured urgency with which our seniors conducted themselves. Afterwards we attended a workshop intended to familiarize us with computer programs such as PowerPoint, Excel, and Access. We spent this class sitting in a semicircle around a soft-spoken instructor who looked like a librarian; Wainwright dubbed it our "Microsoft Family Time."

And finally, in the late afternoon we were divided

into two teams of three for what Sherman referred to as "soft skills training." These sessions involved role-playing real-life situations, such as dealing with an irate client or an uncooperative chief financial officer. We were taught to recognize another person's style of thought, harness their agenda, and redirect it to achieve our desired outcome; indeed one might describe it as a form of mental judo for business.

I see you are impressed by the thoroughness of our training. I was as well. It was a testament to the systematic pragmatism—call it *professionalism*—that underpins your country's success in so many fields. At Princeton, learning was imbued with an aura of creativity; at Underwood Samson, creativity was not excised—it was still present and valued—but it ceded its primacy to *efficiency*. Maximum return was the maxim to which we returned, time and again. We learned to prioritize—to determine the axis on which advancement would be most beneficial—and then to apply ourselves single-mindedly to the achievement of that objective.

But these musings of mine are perhaps rather dry! I do not mean to imply that I did not enjoy my initiation to the realm of high finance. On the contrary, I did. I felt empowered, and besides, all manner of new possibilities were opening up to me. I will give you an example: expense accounts. Do you know how exhilarating it is to be issued a credit card and told that your company will pick up the tab for any ostensibly work-related meal or entertainment? Forgive me: of course you do; you are here, after all, on business. But for me, at the age of twenty-two, this experience was a revelation. I could, if I desired, take my colleagues out for an after-work drink—an activity classified as "new hire cultivation"—and with impunity spend in an hour more than my father earned in a day!

As you can imagine, we new hires availed ourselves of the opportunity to cultivate one another on a regular basis. I remember the first night we did so; we went to the bar at the Royalton, on Forty-Fourth Street. Sherman came with us on this occasion and ordered a bottle of vintage champagne to celebrate our induction. I looked around as we raised our glasses in a toast to ourselves. Two of my five colleagues were women; Wainwright and I were non-white. We were marvelously diverse . . .

and yet we were not: all of us, Sherman included, hailed from the same elite universities—Harvard, Princeton, Stanford, Yale; we all exuded a sense of confident self-satisfaction; and not one of us was either short or overweight.

It struck me then—no, I must be honest, it strikes me *now*—that shorn of hair and dressed in battle fatigues, we would have been virtually indistinguishable. Perhaps something similar had occurred to Wainwright, for he winked and said to me, rather presciently as it would turn out, "Beware the dark side, young Skywalker." He had a penchant for quoting lines from popular cinema, much as my mother quoted the poems of Faiz and Ghalib. But I suspect Wainwright made this particular allusion to *Star Wars* mostly in jest, for immediately afterwards he, like I—like all of us, for that matter—drank heartily.

Sherman left when the champagne was done, but he told us to continue to our hearts' content and to charge our bill to Underwood Samson. We did so, staggering out into the street around midnight. Wainwright and I shared a cab downtown. "Hey man," he said, "do you *get* cricket?" I asked him what he meant. "My dad's nuts about it," he said. "He's from Barbados. West Indies versus Pakistan" —and here he slipped into a Caribbean lilt—"best damn test match I ever saw." I laughed. "That must have been in the eighties," I said. "Neither team is quite so good now."

We were both hungry, and I suggested we stop at the Pak-Punjab Deli. The man behind the counter recognized me; he had given me a free meal that morning when I mentioned it was my first day of work. "My friend," he said, spreading his arms in welcome. "Jenaab," I replied, bowing my head, "do you never go home?" "Not enough," he said. "This time I insist on paying," I told him, unsheathing my credit card and leaning forward—both conspiratorially and drunkenly—to add, "I have an expense account." He shook his head and informed me, to the visible amusement of the exhausted cabdrivers present, that he was sorry, and I could always pay later if I did not have the money, but he did not accept American Express.

Although we were speaking in Urdu, Wainwright seemed to understand. "I have cash," he said. "This stuff looks delicious." I was pleased he thought so; our food, as you have surely gathered in your time here, is something we Lahoris take great pride in. Moreover, it is a mark of friendship when someone treats you to a meal—ushering you thereby into a relationship of mutual generosity—and by the time fifteen minutes later that I saw Wainwright licking his fingers, having dispatched the last crumb on his plate, I knew I had found a kindred spirit at the office.

But why do you recoil? Ah yes, this beggar is a particularly unfortunate fellow. One can only wonder what series of *accidents* could have left him so thoroughly disfigured. He draws close to you because you are a foreigner. Will you give him something? No? Very wise; one ought not to encourage beggars, and yes, you are right, it is far better to donate to charities that address the causes of poverty rather than to him, a creature who is merely its symptom. What am I doing? I am handing him a few rupees—misguidedly, of course, and out of habit. There, he offers us his prayers for our well-being; now he is on his way.

I was telling you about Wainwright. Over the following weeks, it became clear that he was in

strong contention for the top position in our rankings. All of us analyst trainees were competitive
by nature—we had to have been for us to have
acquired the grades necessary for consideration
by Underwood Samson—but Wainwright was less
overtly so; he was genial and irreverent, and was
as a consequence almost universally well-liked. But
there was no doubt in my mind that my friend was
also extremely talented: his presentations were
remarkably clear; he excelled in our interpersonal
exercises; and he had an instinct for identifying what
mattered most in a business case.

I hope you will not think me immodest when I
say that I, too, stood out from the pack. I retained
from my soccer-playing days a sort of controlled
aggression—not belligerence, mind you, but determination—and I harnessed this to my desire to
succeed. How so? Well, I worked hard—harder, I
suspect, than any of the others: subsisting on only a
few hours of sleep a night—and I approached every
class with utter concentration. My tenacity was
frequently commented upon, with approval, by our
instructors. Moreover, my natural politeness and
sense of formality, which had sometimes been a

barrier in my dealings with my peers, proved perfectly suited to the work context in which I now found myself.

I have subsequently wondered why my mannerisms so appealed to my senior colleagues. Perhaps it was my speech: like Pakistan, America is, after all, a former English colony, and it stands to reason, therefore, that an Anglicized accent may in your country continue to be associated with wealth and power, just as it is in mine. Or perhaps it was my ability to function both respectfully and with self-respect in a hierarchical environment, something American youngsters—unlike their Pakistani counterparts—rarely seem trained to do. Whatever the reason, I was aware of an advantage conferred upon me by my foreignness, and I tried to utilize it as much as I could.

My high estimation of Wainwright's and my performance was confirmed when we trainees were divided into two groups of three for our drive to the annual summer party. One group, including Wainwright and me, rode in a limousine with Jim, the managing director who had hired us; the other group rode with Sherman, who, as a vice president,

was more junior in the Underwood Samson pan-
theon. Since nothing at our firm happened by
chance, we all knew this was a sign.

With us in the limousine were some associates
and a vice president from one of Jim's teams.
Everyone began to chat—everyone, that is, except
Jim and myself. Jim observed the conversation in
silence. Then he glanced in my direction, and I
had to avert my eyes so he did not catch *me*
observing *him*. But he continued to look at me in
his steady, penetrating manner until eventually he
said, "You're a watchful guy. You know where
that comes from?" I shook my head. "It comes
from feeling out of place," he said. "Believe me.
I know."

The party was being held at Jim's house in the
Hamptons, a magnificent property that made me
think of *The Great Gatsby*. It was beside the beach—
on a rise behind a protective ridge of sand dunes—
and it had a swimming pool, a tennis court, and an
open-sided white pavilion erected at one end of the
lawn for drinking and dancing. A swing band struck
up as we arrived, and I could smell steak and lobster
being thrown on a grill. Wainwright seemed very

much in his element: he took one of the associates by the arm and soon they were twirling to the beat of the music. The rest of us watched from the sidelines, cocktails in hand.

After a while, I stepped outside the pavilion for some air. The sun had set, and I could see the lights of other houses twinkling in the distance along the curve of the shore. The waves were whispering as they came in, causing me to recall being in Greece not long ago. The sea had always seemed far away to me, luxurious and full of adventure; now it was becoming almost a regular part of my life. How much had changed in the four years since I had left Lahore!

"I remember my first Underwood Samson summer party," a voice said behind me. I turned; it was Jim. He continued, "It was a gorgeous evening, like this one. Barbecue going, music playing. Reminded me of Princeton for some reason, of how I felt when I got there. I figured, I wouldn't mind having a place out in the Hamptons myself one day." I smiled; Jim made one feel he could hear one's thoughts. "I know what you mean," I said. Jim let his gaze wander out over the water, and for a time we stood together in silence. Then he said, "You hungry?" "Yes," I replied. "Good," he said approvingly, and with that he tapped me on either shoulder with the blade of his hand—an odd, deliberate gesture—and led me back inside.

I found myself wishing during the course of the evening that Erica were there. You wondered what had become of her? No, I had not forgotten; she was very much a part of my life in New York, and I shall return to her shortly. For the moment, though, I wanted only to mention in passing that Jim's house was so splendid, I thought even *she* might be impressed. And that, as you will come to understand, is saying a great deal.

A week later, when the analyst training program came to an end, Jim called us one by one to his office. "So," he asked me, "how do you think you did?" "Fairly well," I replied. He laughed. "You did better than fairly well," he said. "You're number one in your class. Your instructors say you've got a bit of the warrior in you. Don't be ashamed of that. Nurture it. It can take you a long way." I was enormously pleased, but I did not know what to say. "I've got a project coming up," Jim went on. "Music business. Philippines. Want to be on it?" "I certainly do," I said. "Thank you."

When I left Jim's office, I found Wainwright waiting for me. "I came second this time," he said, smiling. "I figured you'd be first. And by the way you're glowing, I can see I was right." "I got lucky," I replied. "Not that lucky," he said, putting his arm around my shoulders. "You've got to buy me a drink."

Yes, I was happy in that moment. I felt bathed in a warm sense of accomplishment. Nothing troubled me; I was a young New Yorker with the city at my feet. How soon that would change! My world would be transformed, just as this market around us has been. See how quickly they have brought those tables into the street. Crowds have begun to stroll where only a few minutes ago there was the rumble of traffic. Coming upon this scene now, one might think that Old Anarkali looked *always* thus, regardless of the hour. But we, sir, who have been sitting here for some time, we know better, do we not? Yes, we have acquired a certain familiarity with the recent history of our surroundings, and that—in my humble opinion—allows us to put the present into much better perspective.

4

I see that you have noticed the scar on my forearm, here, where the skin is both darker and smoother than that which surrounds it. I have been told that it looks like a rope burn; my more active friends say it is not dissimilar to marks on the bodies of those who have taken up rappelling—or mountain climbing, for that matter. Perhaps a thought of this nature is passing through *your* mind, for I detect a certain seriousness in your expression, as though you are wondering what sort of training camp could have given a fellow from the plains such as myself cause to engage in these activities!

Allow me, then, to reassure you that the source of my injury was rather prosaic. We have in this country a phenomenon with which you will doubtless be unfamiliar, given the state of plenty that characterizes your homeland. Here—particularly in the winter, when the reservoirs of the great dams are almost dry—we face a shortage of electricity that manifests itself in rolling blackouts. We call this load-shedding, and we keep our homes well-stocked with candles so that it does not unduly disrupt our lives. As a child, during such a time of load-shedding, I grabbed hold of one of these candles, tipped it over, and spilled molten wax on myself. In America, this would have been the start, in all likelihood, of a protracted bout of litigation with the manufacturer for using candle-wax with such a high, and unsafe, melting point; here, it resulted merely in an evening of crying and the rather faint, if oddly linear, scar you see today.

Ah, they have begun to turn on the decorative lights that arc through the air above this market! A little gaudy? Yes, you are right; I myself might have chosen something less colorful. But observe the smiles on the upturned faces of those around us. It is remarkable how *theatrical* manmade light can be once sunlight has begun to fade, how it can affect us emotionally, even now, at the start of the twenty-first century, in cities as large and bright as this one. Think of the expressive beauty of the Empire State Building, illuminated green for St Patrick's

Day, or pale blue on the evening of Frank Sinatra's death. Surely, New York by night must be one of the greatest sights in the world.

I remember my early nocturnal explorations of Manhattan, so often with Erica as my guide. She invited me to her home for dinner soon after our return from Greece; I spent the afternoon deciding what to wear. I knew her family was wealthy, and I wanted to dress as I imagined they would be dressed: in a manner elegant but also casual. My suit seemed too formal; my blazer would have been better, but it was several years old and struck me as somewhat shabby. In the end, I took advantage of the ethnic exception clause that is written into every code of etiquette and wore a starched white kurta of delicately worked cotton over a pair of jeans.

It was a testament to the open-mindedness and—that overused word—*cosmopolitan* nature of New York in those days that I felt completely comfortable on the subway in this attire. Indeed, no one seemed to take much notice of me at all, save for a gay gentleman who politely offered me an invitational smile. I emerged from the 6 train onto

Seventy-Seventh Street, in the heart of the Upper East Side. The area—with its charming bistros, exclusive shops, and attractive women in short skirts walking tiny dogs—felt surprisingly familiar, although I had never been there before; I realized later that I owed my sense of familiarity to the many films that had used it as a setting.

Erica's family lived in an impressive building with a blue canopy and an elderly doorman, who adopted a coldly disapproving expression that would not have been out of place on the face of the gatekeeper of one of Lahore's larger mansions had I driven up in a small and rusted automobile. Naturally, I responded with an equally cold and rather imperious tone—carefully calibrated to convey both that I had taken offense and that I found it beneath myself to say so—as I stated my business. This had its desired effect; he promptly rang up to inquire whether I should be allowed to pass and—when informed that I should—directed me in person to the elevator. I was instructed to press the button for the penthouse, a term associated in my mind with luxury and—yes, I will confess—with pornography as well. So it was in a state of heightened expectation that I arrived at the door of Erica's flat, which opened before I had a chance to knock.

Erica received me with a smile; her tanned skin seemed to glow with health. I had forgotten how stunning she was, and in that moment, pressed as we were into close proximity by the confines of the entryway, I was forced to lower my eyes. "Wow," she said, reaching out to graze the embroidery on my kurta with the tip of her finger, "you look great." I responded that she did, too, which was true, although she was wearing a short Mighty Mouse T-shirt and did not appear to have been quite as preoccupied with issues of dress selection as I had been. She said she wanted to show me something, and I followed her to her bedroom. It was roughly twice the size of my studio flat and contained cartons of university books, a desk with a computer and a laser printer, a massive bed covered with clothes, and a punching bag suspended from the ceiling on a chain; in short, it looked lived-in, the sort of room one has had one's entire life.

I felt a peculiar feeling; I felt at home. Perhaps it was because I had recently lived such a transitory existence—moving from one dorm room to the next—and longed for the settled nature of my past; perhaps it was because I missed my family and the comfort of a family residence, where generations stayed together, instead of apart in an atomized state of age segregation; or perhaps it was because a spacious bedroom in a prestigious apartment on the Upper East Side was, in American terms, the socioeconomic equivalent of a spacious bedroom in a prestigious house in Gulberg, such as the one in which I had grown up. Whatever the reason, it made me smile, and Erica, seeing me smile, smiled back and held up a slender, brown parcel.

"It's done," she said solemnly. I waited for her to say more, and when she did not, I asked, "'It' being?" "My manuscript," she said. "I'm sending it to an agent tomorrow." I took it respectfully in both hands, resting it flat across my upturned palms. "Congratulations," I said, and then, noticing it was rather light, added, "Is this all of it?" She nodded. "It's more a novella than a novel," she said. "It leaves space for your thoughts to echo." I turned it over, appreciating the physicality of the package: the tape which sealed it, the dent in one corner. "Are you nervous?" I asked her. "I'm more unsettled than nervous," she said. "It's like I'm an oyster. I've had this sharp speck inside me for a long time, and I've been trying to make it more comfortable, so slowly I've turned it into a pearl. But now it's finally being taken out, and just as it's going I'm realizing there's a gap being left behind, you know, a dent on my belly where it used to sit. And so I kind of want to hold onto it for a little longer." "Why do you not, then?" I asked, returning it to her. "I already have," she said, and she smiled again. "It's been lying in this envelope since before we went to Greece."

I was honored and pleased that she was confiding in me in this fashion. I met her eyes, and for the first time I perceived that there was something *broken* behind them, like a tiny crack in a diamond that becomes visible only when viewed through a magnifying lens; normally it is hidden by the brilliance of the stone. I wanted to know what it was, what had caused her to create the pearl of which she had spoken. But I thought it would be presumptuous of me to ask; such things are revealed by a person when and to whom they choose. So I attempted to convey through my expression alone my desire to understand her and said nothing further.

As we were leaving her room, I noticed a sketch on the wall. It depicted under stormy skies a tropical island with a runway and a steep volcano; nestled in the caldera of the volcano was a lake with another, smaller island in it—an island on an island—wonderfully sheltered and calm. "What is this?" I asked. "Chris did it," she replied, "when we were eight or nine. It's inspired by one of his Tintin comics, *Flight 714*." "It is beautiful," I said. She nodded. "Yeah," she said, "it is. His mother gave it to me when she was clearing out his stuff." I looked at it a moment longer, fascinated by the intricacy of the pencil-work. In its attention to detail—though not, of course, in its style or subject—it reminded me of our miniature paintings, of the sort one would find if one ventured around the corner to the Lahore Museum or the National College of Arts.

Erica led me outside to their roof terrace—a private aerie with a spectacular, eagle's-eye view of Manhattan—and introduced me to her parents. Her mother was sitting at a table-tennis table that had been converted with four place settings into the venue for our dinner; she held my hand, said hello, and then, still holding my hand, added approvingly to Erica, "Very nice." "Behave, Mom," Erica replied. Her father stood at a grill, placing hamburgers onto plates; it was apparent from his demeanor that he was a man of consequence in the corporate world. As we took our seats for the meal, he lifted a bottle of red wine and said to me, "You drink?" "He's twenty-two," Erica's mother said on my behalf, in a tone that suggested, *So of course he drinks*. "I had a Pakistani working for me once," Erica's father said. "Never drank." "I do, sir," I assured him. "Thank you."

You seem puzzled by this—and not for the first time. Perhaps you misconstrue the significance of my beard, which, I should in any case make clear, I had not yet kept when I arrived in New York. In truth, many Pakistanis drink; alcohol's illegality in our country has roughly the same effect as marijuana's in yours. Moreover, not all of our drinkers are western-educated urbanites such as myself; our newspapers regularly carry accounts of villagers dying or going blind after consuming poor-quality moonshine. Indeed, in our poetry and folk songs *intoxication* occupies a recurring role as a facilitator of love and spiritual enlightenment. What? Is it not a sin? Yes, it certainly is—and so, for that matter, is coveting thy neighbor's wife. I see you smile; we understand one another, then.

But I digress. I was telling you of my first meal with Erica's family. It was a warm evening, like this one—summer in New York being like spring here in Lahore. A breeze was blowing then, again as it is now, and it carried a smell of flame-cooked meat not dissimilar to that coming to us from the many open-air restaurants in this market that are beginning their preparations for dinner. The setting was superb, the wine was delicious, the burgers were succulent, and our conversation was for the most part rather pleasant. Erica seemed happy that I was there, and her happiness infected me as well.

I do, however, remember becoming annoyed at one point in the discussion. Erica's father had asked me how things were back home, and I had replied that they were quite good, thank you, when he said, "Economy's falling apart though, no? Corruption, dictatorship, the rich living like princes while everyone else suffers. Solid people, don't get me wrong. I like Pakistanis. But the elite has raped that place well and good, right? And fundamentalism. You guys have got some serious problems with fundamentalism."

I felt myself bridle. There was nothing overtly objectionable in what he had said; indeed, his was a summary with some knowledge, much like the short news items on the front page of *The Wall Street Journal*, which I had recently begun to read. But his tone—with, if you will forgive me, its typically *American* undercurrent of condescension—struck a negative chord with me, and it was only out of politeness that I limited my response to, "Yes, there are challenges, sir, but my family is there, and I can assure you it is not as bad as that."

Fortunately, the remainder of our dinner passed without incident. Afterwards Erica and I shared a taxi down to Chelsea, where a friend of hers— the daughter of the owner of a contemporary art gallery—had invited her to a party to celebrate the opening of a show. I could hear our driver chatting on his mobile in Punjabi and knew from his accent that he was Pakistani. Normally I would have said hello, but on that particular night I did not. Erica was watching me with considerable curiosity; eventually she remarked, "I hope you're not still upset about what my dad said." "Upset?" I responded. "Of course not. Not in the least." She laughed. "You're a terrible liar," she said. "You're touchy about where you come from. It shows on your face." "Then I apologize," I said. "I had no right to be rude." "You're never rude," she said, smiling, "and I think it's good to be touchy sometimes. It means you care."

We alighted on West Twenty-Fourth Street. I insisted on paying for our cab, and Erica led me by the hand into an unimpressive building, a decrepit, post-industrial hulk. Upon entering I heard music; it grew louder as we mounted several flights of stairs, until finally we pushed open a fire door and were immersed in sound. The gallery was a vast space, white, with clean lines and minimalist fixtures; video projections of faces glowed on the blank heads of mannequins. I realized I was being ushered into an insider's world—the chic heart of this city—to which I would otherwise have had no access. We passed fashion models, old men with tans, artists in outrageous outfits; I was glad I had worn my kurta.

Erica was soon at the center of a circle of friends, none of whom I had previously met. I watched as she attracted people to her, and I was reminded of our trip to Greece, of the *gravity* she had exerted on our group. Yet this time was different; this time she had brought me with her, and she made certain— through a glance, the offer of a drink, the touch of her hand at my elbow—that we remained connected throughout the evening. When she kissed me on the cheek hours later, as I held the door of the cab in which she would return to her home alone, I felt as though we had spent an intimate evening together, even though we had spoken little at the party. Perhaps she felt the same, for at that very instant she said, "Thank you." I was taken by surprise; I thought I should be thanking her, but I had no time to say so, because she pulled the door shut and then she was gone.

In the weeks that followed, she did invite me to meet her on a number of occasions. But unlike that first night—when we were together in her room and in the taxi—we were never again alone.

We went to a small music venue on the Lower East Side, a French restaurant in the meatpacking district, a loft party in TriBeCa—but always in the company of others. Often, I found myself observing Erica as she stood or sat, surrounded by her acquaintances. At these moments she frequently became introspective; it was as though their presence allowed her to withdraw, to recede a half-step inside herself. She reminded me of a child who could sleep only with the door open and the light on.

Sometimes she would become aware of my gaze upon her, and then she would smile at me as though—or so I flattered myself to believe—I had placed a shawl around her shoulders as she returned from a walk in the cold. We exchanged only pleasantries on these outings, and yet I felt our relationship was deepening. At the end of the evening she would kiss my cheek, and it seemed to me that she lingered a fraction longer each time, until her kisses lasted long enough for me to catch a trace of her scent and perceive the softness of the indentation at the corner of her mouth.

My patience was rewarded the weekend before I left for Manila, when Erica asked me to join her for a picnic lunch in Central Park and I discovered that we were not to be met by anyone else. It was one of those glorious late-July afternoons in New York when a stiff wind off the Atlantic makes the trees swell and the clouds race across the sky. You know them well? Yes, precisely: the humidity vanishes as the city fills its lungs with cooler, briny air. Erica wore a straw hat and carried a wicker basket containing wine, fresh-baked bread, sliced meats, several different cheeses, and grapes—a delicious and, to my mind, rather sophisticated assortment.

We chatted as we ate, lounging in the grass. "Do people have picnics in Lahore?" she asked me. "Not so much in the summer," I told her. "At least not if they have any choice in the matter. The sun is too strong, and the only people one sees sitting outside are clustered in the shade." "So this must seem very foreign to you, then," she said. "No," I replied, "in fact it reminds me of when my family would go up to Nathia Galli, in the foothills of the Himalayas. There we often used to take our meals in the open—with tea and cucumber sandwiches from the hotel." She smiled at the image, then became thoughtful and fell silent.

"I haven't done this in a long time," she told me when she spoke again. "Chris and I used to come to the park a lot. We'd bring this basket with us and just read or hang out for hours." "Was it when he died," I asked, "that you stopped coming?" "I stopped," she answered, plucking a daisy, "a bunch of things. For a while I stopped talking to people. I stopped eating. I had to go to the hospital. They told me not to think about it so much and put me on medication. My mom had to take three months off work because I couldn't be by myself. We kept it quiet, though, and by September I was back at Princeton."

That was all she said, and she said it in a normal, if quiet, voice. But I glimpsed again—even more clearly than before—the crack inside her; it evoked in me an almost familial tenderness. When we got up to depart, I offered her my arm and she smiled as she accepted it. Then the two of us walked off, leaving Central Park behind. I remember vividly the feeling of her skin, cool and smooth, on mine. We had never before remained in contact for such a prolonged period; the sensation that her body was so strong and yet belonged to someone so wounded lingered with me until long afterwards. Indeed, weeks later, in my hotel room in Manila, I would at times wake up to that sensation as though touched by a ghost.

What bad luck! The lights have gone. But why do you leap to your feet? Do not be alarmed, sir; as I mentioned before, fluctuations and blackouts are common in Pakistan. Really, you are overreacting; it is not yet so dark. The sky above us still contains a tinge of color, and I can see you quite clearly as you stand there with your hand in your jacket. I assure you: no one will attempt to steal your wallet. For a city of this size, Lahore is remarkably free of that sort of petty crime. Do sit down, I implore you, or you shall force me to stand as well. As it is, I feel rude to remain in this position while my guest is uncomfortable.

Ah, they are back! Thank goodness. It was nothing more than a momentary disruption. And you—to jump as though you were a mouse suddenly under the shadow of a hawk! I would offer you a whiskey to settle your nerves, if only I could. A Jack Daniel's, eh? You smile; I have hit upon a spirit to which you are partial. Sadly, all the beverages in this market that can trace their origin to your country are carbonated soft drinks. One of those will do? Then I will summon our waiter immediately.

5

Observe, sir: bats have begun to appear in the air above this square. Creepy, you say? What a delightfully American expression—one I have not heard in many years! I do not find them creepy; indeed, I quite like them. They remind me of when I was younger; they would swoop at us as we swam in my grandfather's pool, perhaps mistaking us for frogs. Lahore was home to even larger creatures of the night back then—flying foxes, my father used to call them—and when we drove along Mall Road in the evenings we would see them hanging upside down from the canopies of the oldest trees. They are gone now; it is possible that, like butterflies and fireflies, they belonged to a *dreamier* world incompatible with the pollution and congestion of a modern metropolis. Today, one glimpses them only in the surrounding countryside.

But bats have survived here. They are successful

urban dwellers, like you and I, swift enough to escape detection and canny enough to hunt among a crowd. I marvel at their ability to navigate the cityscape; no matter how close they come to these buildings, they are never involved in a collision. Butterflies, on the other hand, tend to splatter on the windshields of passing automobiles, and I have once seen a firefly bumping repeatedly against the window of a house, unable to comprehend the glass that barred its way. Maybe flying foxes lacked the radar—or the agility—of their smaller cousins and therefore hurtled to their deaths against Lahore's newer offices and plazas—structures that rose higher than any had before. If so, they would have long been extinct in New York—or even in Manila, for that matter!

When I arrived in the Philippines at the start of my first Underwood Samson assignment, I was terribly excited. We had flown first class, and I will never forget the feeling of reclining in my seat, clad in my suit, as I was served champagne by an attractive and—yes, I was indeed so brazen as to allow myself to believe—*flirtatious* flight attendant. I was, in my own eyes, a veritable James Bond—

only younger, darker, and possibly better paid. How odd it seems now to recall that time; how quickly my sense of self-satisfaction would later disappear!

But I am getting ahead of myself. I was telling you about Manila. Have you been to the East, sir? You have! Truly, you are well-traveled for an American—for a person of any country, for that matter. I am increasingly curious as to the nature of your *business*—but I am certain you will tell me in due course; for the moment you seem to prefer that I continue. Since you have been to the East, you do not need me to explain how prodigious are the changes taking place in that part of the globe. I expected to find a city like Lahore—or perhaps Karachi; what I found instead was a place of sky-scrapers and superhighways. Yes, Manila had its slums; one saw them on the drive from the airport: vast districts of men in dirty white undershirts lounging idly in front of auto-repair shops—like a poorer version of the 1950s America depicted in such films as *Grease*. But Manila's glittering skyline and walled enclaves for the ultra-rich were unlike anything I had seen in Pakistan.

I tried not to dwell on the comparison; it was one

thing to accept that New York was more wealthy
than Lahore, but quite another to swallow the fact
that Manila was as well. I felt like a distance runner
who thinks he is not doing too badly until he
glances over his shoulder and sees that the fellow
who is lapping him is not the leader of the pack, but
one of the laggards. Perhaps it was for this reason
that I did something in Manila I had never done
before: I attempted to act and speak, as much as
my dignity would permit, more like an *American*.
The Filipinos we worked with seemed to look up
to my American colleagues, accepting them almost
instinctively as members of the officer class of global
business—and I wanted my share of that respect
as well.

So I learned to tell executives my father's age,
"I need it *now*"; I learned to cut to the front of
lines with an extraterritorial smile; and I learned
to answer, when asked where I was from, that I
was from New York. Did these things trouble me,
you ask? Certainly, sir; I was often ashamed. But
outwardly I gave no sign of this. In any case, there
was much for me to be proud of: my genuine
aptitude for our work, for example, and the glow-

ing reviews my performance received from my peers.

We were there, as I mentioned to you earlier, to value a recorded-music business. The owner had been a legendary figure in the local A&R scene; when he removed his sunglasses, his eyes contained the sort of cosmic openness one associates with prolonged exposure to LSD. But despite his colorful past, he had managed to sign lucrative outsourcing deals to manufacture and distribute CDs for two of the international music majors. Indeed, he claimed his operation was the largest of its kind in Southeast Asia and—piracy, downloads, and Chinese competition notwithstanding—growing at quite a healthy clip.

To determine how much it was actually worth, we worked around the clock for over a month. We interviewed suppliers, employees, and experts of all kinds; we passed hours in closed rooms with accountants and lawyers; we gathered gigabytes of data; we compared indicators of performance to benchmarks; and, in the end, we built a complex financial model with innumerable permutations. I spent much of my time in front of my computer, but I also visited the factory floor and several music shops. I felt enormously powerful on these outings, knowing my team was shaping the future. Would these workers be fired? Would these CDs be made elsewhere? *We,* indirectly of course, would help decide.

Yet there were moments when I became disoriented. I remember one such occasion in particular. I was riding with my colleagues in a limousine. We were mired in traffic, unable to move, and I glanced out the window to see, only a few feet away, the driver of a jeepney returning my gaze. There was an undisguised hostility in his expression; I had no idea why. We had not met before—of that I was virtually certain—and in a few minutes we would probably never see one another again. But his dislike was so obvious, so *intimate,* that it got under my skin. I stared back at him, getting angry myself—you will have noticed in your time here that glaring is something we men of Lahore take seriously—and I maintained eye contact until he was obliged by the movement of the car in front to return his attention to the road.

Afterwards, I tried to understand why he acted as he did. Perhaps, I thought, his wife has just left him; perhaps he resents me for the privileges implied by my suit and expensive car; perhaps he simply does not like Americans. I remained preoccupied with this matter far longer than I should have, pursuing several possibilities that all assumed—as their unconscious starting point—that he and I shared a sort of Third World sensibility. Then one of my colleagues asked me a question, and when I turned to answer him, something rather strange took place. I looked at him—at his fair hair and light eyes and, most of all, his oblivious immersion in the minutiae of our work—and thought, you are so *foreign*. I felt in that moment much closer to the Filipino driver than to him; I felt I was play-acting when in reality I ought to be making my way home, like the people on the street outside.

I did not say anything, of course, but I was sufficiently unsettled by this peculiar series of events—or impressions, really, for they hardly constituted *events*—that I found it difficult to sleep that night. Fortunately, however, the intensity of our assignment did not permit me to indulge in further bouts of insomnia; the next day I was at the office until two in the morning, and when I returned to my hotel room, I slept like a baby.

During my time in Manila—I arrived in late July and left in mid-September—my main links to friends and family were weekly phone calls to Lahore and online correspondence with Erica in New York. Because of the time difference, messages she wrote in the morning arrived in my inbox in the evening, and I looked forward to reading and replying to them before I went to bed. Her emails were invariably brief; she never wrote more than a paragraph or two. But she managed to say a great deal with few words. One note, for example, contained something to the effect of: "C.—I'm in the Hamptons. A bunch of us were hanging out on the beach today and I went for a walk by myself. I found this rock pool. Do you like rock pools? I love them. They're like little worlds. Perfect, self-contained, transparent. They look like they're frozen in time. Then the tide rises and a wave crashes in and they start all over again with new fish left behind. Anyway when I got back everyone kept asking where I'd been and I realized

I'd spent the entire afternoon there. It was kind of surreal. Made me think of you.—E."

Such messages were enough to lift my spirits for several days. Perhaps this strikes you as an exaggeration. But you must understand that in Lahore, at least when I was in secondary school—youngsters here, like everywhere else, are probably more liberated now—relationships were often conducted over fleeting phone calls, messages through friends, and promises of encounters that never happened. Many parents were strict, and sometimes weeks would pass without us being able to meet those we thought of as our girlfriends. So we learned to *savor* the denial of gratification—that most un-American of pleasures!—and I for one could subsist quite happily on a diet of emails such as that which I have just described.

But I was of course eager to see Erica again and was therefore in high spirits as our project approached its end. Jim had flown in to satisfy himself with our final conclusions; he sat me down for a drink. "So, Changez," he said, taking in our exquisite hotel, the Makati Shangri-La, with a sweep of his hand, "getting used to all this?" "I am indeed, sir," I replied. "Everyone's saying great things about you," he said, pausing to see how I responded; when I smiled, he went on, "Except that you're working too hard. You don't want to burn out, now." "Allow me to reassure you," I said. "I get more than enough rest." He raised an eyebrow and started to laugh. "I like you, you know that?" he said. "Really. Not in a bullshit, say-something-nice-to-raise-the-kid's-morale way. You're a shark. And that's a compliment, coming from me. It's what they called me when I first joined. A shark. I never stopped swimming. And I was a cool customer. I never let on that I felt like I didn't belong to this world. Just like you."

It was not the first time Jim had spoken to me in this fashion; I was always uncertain of how to respond. The confession that implicates its audience is—as we say in cricket—a devilishly difficult ball to play. Reject it and you slight the confessor; accept it and you admit your own guilt. So I said, rather carefully, "Why did you not belong?" He smiled—again as if he could see right through me—and replied, "Because I grew up on the other side. For half my life, I was outside the candy store look-

ing in, kid. And in America, no matter how poor
you are, TV gives you a good view. But I was dirt
poor. My dad died of gangrene. So I get the irony
of paying a hundred bucks for a bottle of fermented
grape juice, if you know what I mean."

I thought about this. As I have already told you,
I did not grow up in poverty. But I did grow up
with a poor boy's sense of *longing,* in my case not
for what my family had never had, but for what we
had had and lost. Some of my relatives held onto
imagined memories the way homeless people hold
onto lottery tickets. *Nostalgia* was their crack
cocaine, if you will, and my childhood was littered
with the consequences of their addiction: unservice-
able debts, squabbles over inheritances, the odd
alcoholic or suicide. In this, Jim and I were indeed
similar: he had grown up outside the candy store,
and I had grown up on its threshold as its door
was being shut.

We were joined at the bar by other members
of the team, but Jim sat with his arm around the
back of my chair in a way that made me feel—quite
literally—as though he had taken me under his
wing. It was a good feeling, and it felt even better

when I saw how the hotel staff were responding to him; they had identified Jim as a man of substance, and the smiles and attention he received were impressive to behold. I was the only non-American in our group, but I suspected my Pakistaniness was invisible, cloaked by my suit, by my expense account, and—most of all—by my companions.

And yet . . . No, I ought to pause here, for I think you will find rather unpalatable what I intend to say next, and I wish to warn you before I proceed. Besides, my throat is parched; the breeze seems to have disappeared entirely and, although night has fallen, it is still rather warm. Would you care for another soft drink? No? You are curious, you say, and desire me to continue? Very well. I will just signal our waiter to bring a bottle for me; there, it is done. And here he comes, making such haste; one would think we were his only customers! Ah, delicious: this is precisely what I required.

The following evening was supposed to be our last in Manila. I was in my room, packing my things. I turned on the television and saw what at first I took to be a film. But as I continued to watch, I realized that it was not fiction but news. I stared as one—and then the other—of the twin towers of New York's World Trade Center collapsed. And then I *smiled*. Yes, despicable as it may sound, my initial reaction was to be remarkably pleased.

Your disgust is evident; indeed, your large hand has, perhaps without your noticing, clenched into a fist. But please believe me when I tell you that I am no sociopath; I am not indifferent to the suffering of others. When I hear of an acquaintance who has been diagnosed with a serious illness, I feel—almost without fail—a sympathetic pain, a twinge in my kidneys strong enough to elicit a wince. When I am approached for a donation to charity, I tend to be forthcoming, at least insofar as my modest means will permit. So when I tell you I was pleased at the slaughter of thousands of innocents, I do so with a profound sense of perplexity.

But at that moment, my thoughts were not with the *victims* of the attack—death on television moves me most when it is fictitious and happens to characters with whom I have built up relationships over multiple episodes—no, I was caught up in the *symbolism* of it all, the fact that someone had so visibly brought America to her knees. Ah, I see I am only compounding your displeasure. I understand, of course; it is hateful to hear another person gloat over one's country's misfortune. But surely you cannot be completely innocent of such feelings yourself. Do you feel no joy at the video clips—so prevalent these days—of American munitions laying waste the structures of your enemies?

But you are at war, you say? Yes, you have a point. I was not at war with America. Far from it: I was the product of an American university; I was earning a lucrative American salary; I was infatuated with an American woman. So why did part of me desire to see America harmed? I did not know, then; I knew merely that my feelings would be unacceptable to my colleagues, and I undertook to hide them as well as I could. When my team gathered in Jim's room later that evening, I feigned the same shock and anguish I saw on the faces around me.

But hearing them speak of their loved ones, my thoughts turned to Erica, and I no longer needed to pretend. I did not yet know, of course, that the dying was confined to the limited geography of what would come to be called Ground Zero. Nor did I yet know that Erica was safely at home when the attacks took place. I was almost relieved to be worried for her and unable to sleep; this allowed me to share in the anxiety of my colleagues and ignore for a time my initial sense of pleasure.

We were unable to leave Manila for several days, on account of flights being canceled. At the airport, I was escorted by armed guards into a room where I was made to strip down to my boxer shorts—I had, rather embarrassingly, chosen to wear a pink pair patterned with teddy bears, but their revelation had no impact on the severe expressions of my inspectors—and I was, as a consequence, the last person to board our aircraft. My entrance elicited looks of concern from many of my fellow passengers. I flew to New York uncomfortable in my own face: I was aware of being under suspicion; I felt guilty; I tried therefore to be as nonchalant as possible; this naturally led to my becoming stiff and self-conscious. Jim, who was sitting next to me, asked on multiple occasions if I was all right.

When we arrived, I was separated from my team at immigration. They joined the queue for American citizens; I joined the one for foreigners. The officer who inspected my passport was a solidly built woman with a pistol at her hip and a mastery of English inferior to mine; I attempted to disarm her with a smile. "What is the purpose of your trip to the United States?" she asked me. "I live here," I replied. "That is *not* what I asked you, sir," she said. "What is the *purpose* of your trip to the United States?" Our exchange continued in much this fashion for several minutes. In the end I was dispatched for a secondary inspection in a room where I sat on a metal bench next to a tattooed man in handcuffs. My team did not wait for me; by the time I entered the customs hall they had already collected their suitcases and left. As a consequence, I rode to Manhattan that evening very much alone.

But why do you flinch? Ah yes, the bats; they are circling rather low. They will not touch us; allow me to reassure you on that score. You know, you say? Your tone is curt; I can see that I have offended you, *angered* you even. But I have not, I suspect, entirely *surprised* you. Do you deny it? No? And *that* is of not inconsiderable interest to me, for we have not met before, and yet you seem to know at least something about me. Perhaps you have drawn certain conclusions from my appearance, my lustrous beard; perhaps you have merely followed the arc of my tale with the uncanny skill of a skeet shooter; or perhaps ... But enough of these speculations! Let us cast our gaze over a menu; I have spoken too much, and I fear I have been negligent in my duties as a host. Besides, I wish now to hear more of *you:* what brings you to Lahore, what company you work for, et cetera, et cetera. Night is deepening around us, and despite the lights above this market, your face is mostly in shadow. Let us, like the bats, exercise our other senses, since our eyes are of diminishing utility. Your ears must be exhausted; the time has come to employ your tongue—for taste, if nothing more, although I hope you can be persuaded to speak!

6

You hesitate, sir; I did not mean to put you on the spot. If you are not yet ready to reveal your *purpose* in traveling here—your demeanor all but precludes the possibility that you are a tourist wandering aimlessly through this part of the world—then I will not insist. Ah, I see that you have detected a scent. Nothing escapes you; your senses are as acute as those of a fox in the wild. It is rather pleasant, is it not? Yes, you are right: it *is* jasmine. It comes, as your glance suggests you have already surmised, from the table beside ours, where that family has just taken their seats for dinner.

What a contrast: the paleness of those buds—strung with needle and thread into a fluffy bracelet—against the darkness of that lady's skin! And what a contrast, again: the delicacy of their perfume against the robust smell of roasting meat! It is remarkable indeed how we human beings are capable of delighting in the mating call of a flower while we are surrounded by the charred carcasses of our fellow animals—but then we are remarkable creatures. Perhaps it is in our nature to recognize subconsciously the link between mortality and procreation—between, that is to say, the finite and the infinite—and we are in fact driven by reminders of the one to seek out the other.

I remember being tasked with purchasing such flowers upon the death of my maternal grandmother. I was sixteen at the time and in possession of a fake motor vehicle learner's permit—it had been my brother's—and I was so excited to be behind the wheel of an automobile that I was regularly sent by my family to do errands that might otherwise have been carried out by our chauffeur. Our Toyota Corolla was lovingly maintained but getting on in years and therefore prone—as happened in this particular case—to overheating. To this day I can still recall the heady aroma of those strands of threaded jasmine piled high in my arms as I walked to the cemetery, sweating in the summer sun.

New York was in mourning after the destruction

of the World Trade Center, and floral motifs figured
prominently in the shrines to the dead and the
missing that had sprung up in my absence. I would
often glance at them as I walked by: photos,
bouquets, words of condolence—nestled into street
corners and between shops and along the railings
of public squares. They reminded me of my own
uncharitable—indeed, inhumane—response to the
tragedy, and I felt from them a constant murmur
of reproach.

Other reproaches were far louder. Your country's
flag invaded New York after the attacks; it was
everywhere. Small flags stuck on toothpicks featured
in the shrines; stickers of flags adorned windshields
and windows; large flags fluttered from buildings.
They all seemed to proclaim: *We are America*—not
New York, which, in my opinion, means something quite different—*the mightiest civilization the
world has ever known; you have slighted us; beware our
wrath*. Gazing up at the soaring towers of the city,
I wondered what manner of host would sally forth
from so grand a castle.

It was against this backdrop that I saw Erica again.
Six weeks had passed since that afternoon we spent

together in Central Park, and when I called I thought Erica might have other plans, but she suggested we meet that very evening, which is to say the evening of my first full day back in New York, as soon as I was done with work. I was waiting on the sidewalk as she stepped out of a taxi. A peculiar odor lingered in the air; the smoldering wreckage downtown made its way into our lungs. Her lips were pale, as though she had not slept— or perhaps she had been crying. I thought in that moment that she looked older, more elegant; she had an element of that beauty which only age can confer upon a woman, and I imagined I was catching a glimpse of the Erica she would one day become. Truly, I thought, she is an empress-in-waiting!

"My mom was saying," she said over dinner, "maybe we should leave the city for a bit. Go out to the Hamptons. But I told her the last thing I wanted to do was leave town. I didn't want to be alone. The attacks churned up old thoughts in my head." I nodded but said nothing in response. I felt we were encountering one another at a funeral; one never knows what to say to those who have been bereaved. "I keep thinking about Chris," she went on. "I don't know why. Most nights I have to take something to help me rest. It's kind of like I've been thrown back a year." I suspect I looked alarmed because she smiled and added, "It's not *that* bad. I mean, I'm eating fine. I haven't lost it. But I feel haunted, you know?"

I considered her choice of words. "I have an aunt," I said, "my mother's most beautiful sister. Her marriage was arranged, so she had only met her husband a few times beforehand. He was an air force pilot. He died three months later, but she never married again. She said he was the love of her life." Erica appeared moved, both touched and troubled by what I had said; leaning forward, she asked, "What's she like now?" "Mad," I said, "mad as a March hare." Erica stared; then she started to laugh—a surprised and delighted guffaw—and when she was done she placed her hand on mine. "I missed you," she said. "It's good to have you back."

I wanted to slip my fingers between hers, but I held my hand completely still, as though I was afraid any movement on my part might dislodge our connection. "Is she really mad?" Erica asked, raising an eyebrow and imitating my pronunciation of the word. "Yes, I am afraid," I said with mock solemnity, "utterly." This made her smile; she suggested we order another bottle of wine. We lingered at our table until the restaurant closed for the night—by which time we were rather pleasantly drunk—and then strolled out into the street. "I love it when you talk about where you come from," she said, slipping her arm through mine, "you become so *alive*."

I did not say that the same could be said of her when she spoke of Chris; I did not say it because this fact elicited in me mixed emotions. On the one hand it pleased me as her friend to see her so animated, and I knew, moreover, that it was a mark of affection that she took me into her confidence in this way—I had never heard her discuss Chris when speaking to someone else; on the other hand, I was desirous of embarking upon a relationship with her that amounted to more than friendship, and I felt in the strength of her ongoing attachment to Chris the presence of a rival—albeit a dead one—with whom I feared I could never compete. The aunt I had mentioned was unlike Erica in almost every way: she was plump, insisted on traveling only by scooter, wore a backpack frequently crammed with goodies for her young nieces and nephews, and lived on a widow's small pension. But this was my aunt at forty-five; the woman who stared jauntily out of her photographs at the age of twenty-two was cocksure and painfully attractive. I could only imagine how many suitors she had turned away, and I wondered if my infatuation with Erica was as doomed as theirs had been.

Erica's face was relaxed now; indeed she stifled a yawn as she leaned her head against my shoulder. But she had been tense at the start of the evening, careworn and riddled with worry. Like so many others in the city after the attacks, she appeared deeply anxious. Yet her anxieties seemed only indirectly related to the prospect of dying at the hands of terrorists. The destruction of the World Trade Center had, as she had said, churned up old thoughts that had settled in the manner of sediment to the bottom of a pond; now the waters of her mind were murky with what previously had been ignored. I did not know if the same was true of me.

We wandered in silence through the night, and as luck would have it—no, I am being dishonest; luck had nothing to do with it—we found ourselves outside my building. "Can I come up?" she asked. "I want to see where you live." I could hear my heart beating as we mounted the stairs; my studio was a fourth-floor walkup so, as you can well imagine, there were a great many to climb. I was somewhat apprehensive of what she might think of the place—it was, after all, a tiny fraction of the size of her own home—but I reassured myself that it possessed a certain *literary* charm. "It's perfect," she said, sitting down on the edge of my futon, which was at that moment still in its extended position for use as a bed.

She shut her eyes, leaned back on her elbows, and smiled drowsily, in the manner of a trusting little girl. My bladder was dangerously close to bursting, and before dashing off to the lavatory I informed her I would return immediately. By the time I emerged, she was fast asleep. "Erica?" I said. There was no answer. I did not know what to do, and hesitated before eventually turning off the light. The blinds were up; the nighttime glow of Manhattan found its way inside, and I watched the gentle rise and fall of her chest as she breathed. Then I covered her with a sheet and tossed a pillow on the floor for myself. I was exhausted, and suffering from jet lag in addition, but I had long to wait before dreams took me. I did not wake in the morning when, as I later learned, she kissed me on the forehead before leaving.

But observe! A flower-seller approaches. I will summon him to our table. You are not in the mood? Surely you cannot object to a single strand of jasmine buds. Here, take them in your hand: are they not like balls of velvet in their texture? More like popcorn shrimp, you say? Ah, you jest; for an instant I thought you were being serious. Yet you have succeeded in reminding me of a delicacy we entirely lack in Lahore, being so far from the sea. What I would not give for a bucket of American popcorn shrimp—fried in batter until a delicious golden-brown and served with a sachet of tomato sauce!—but sadly, I will have to content myself with these flowers instead: so rare in New York, so common here.

Where was I? Yes, I was telling you of Erica and my return to New York. After she had slept at my flat, Erica took to inviting me out with pleasing regularity. I accompanied her to fundraisers for the victims of the World Trade Center, dinners at the houses—for they *were* houses, brownstones preserved as islands of single-family accommodation amidst Manhattan's sea of apartments—of her friends, openings and private viewings for patrons of the arts. I became, in effect, her official escort at the events of New York society.

This role pleased me indeed. I was presumptuous enough to think that this was how my life was *meant* to be, that it had in some way been inevitable that I should end up rubbing shoulders with the truly wealthy in such exalted settings. Erica vouched for my worthiness; my way of carrying myself—I flattered myself to believe—suggested the impeccability of my breeding; and, for those who inquired further, my Princeton degree and Underwood Samson business card were invariably sufficient to earn me a respectful nod of approval.

Looking back now, I see there was a certain symmetry to the situation: I felt I was entering in New York the very same social class that my family was falling out of in Lahore. Perhaps this accounted for a good part of the comfort and satisfaction I found in my new environment. But an even greater part of my happiness in those days was due to being in the regular company of Erica. I could, without exaggeration, watch her for hours. The pride of her stance, the slender muscularity of her arms and shoulders, the failure of her garments to cloak the memory of those naked breasts I had seen in Greece: all these things filled me with desire.

And yet I was also filled with protectiveness. Often, as we stood or sat in the midst of an impeccably turned-out crowd, I would observe that she was utterly detached, lost in a world of her own. Her eyes were turned inward, and remarks made by her companions would register only indirectly on her face, like the shadows of clouds gliding across the surface of a lake. She smiled when it was brought to her attention that she seemed distant, and said she was, as usual, *spacing out*. But I had come to suspect that hers were not merely the lapses of the absent-minded; no, she was struggling against a current that pulled her within herself, and her smile contained the fear that she might slip into her own depths, where she would be trapped, unable to breathe. I wished to serve as her anchor in these moments, without being so vulgar as to make known to her that this was a role I felt she needed someone to play. I discovered that the best way of doing this was to come close to touching her—to rest my hand on a table, say, as near as possible to hers without actually making contact—and then to wait for her to become aware of my physical presence, at which point she would shake her head as if waking from a dream and bridge the gap between us with a small caress.

Perhaps it was this sense of protectiveness that prevented my attempting to kiss Erica; equally likely, it was the shyness and awe that accompany first love. In any case, several weeks passed before one night, after a Burmese meal in the East Village, Erica held me back as her friends hailed taxis and began to disperse. "I have something to tell you," she said. "I want to celebrate." "Why?" I asked. "Because," she said, pressing her fingertips together and smiling broadly, "I got an agent!" Her initial blind submissions had been unsuccessful, she explained, but she had recently sent her manuscript to an agency that represented a family friend; a junior

·

agent there had just this afternoon agreed to take her on. He said length had been his only concern—the novella form being, in his words, a platypus of a beast—but upon reflection he thought he could make a strong case to publishers. I congratulated her and said I would most willingly accompany her on any adventure she chose for the evening; she suggested we purchase a magnum of champagne and proceed to my flat, which was just around the corner.

She said this as though it was the most natural thing in the world; I smiled assent in—as best I could manage—the same easy manner. But it was clear to both of us, I think it safe to say, that a certain *gravity* had attached itself to our actions, and I for one was uncharacteristically clumsy as I searched in my pocket, first in a liquor store for change, and later on the steps in front of my building for my keys. It was a nippy October day and Erica was dressed warmly; indoors, she removed her sleeveless jacket and her cotton sweater, shedding layers until she achieved her preferred attire of T-shirt and jeans. Lacking a candle, I turned on my television and set it to mute, thereby bathing the room in a dim, flickering light. We drank from a pair of ornate silver cups that had been a graduation present from one of my uncles; the effect was to make the champagne taste metallic, but in a not unpleasant—and indeed rather exotic—fashion.

"I got banged up at tae kwon do practice today," Erica said. "We were sparring, and I was up against this woman who's really quick. She nailed me right under the armpit. Here," she touched herself, "I can feel it when I breathe. It's a pretty good bruise." She looked at me. I fingered my knee, following the scar left by my surgery. Then Erica said, "Do you want to see it?" I watched her, trying to determine whether she was joking; she did not seem to be. So I nodded, at that moment unable to trust my voice. I had thought she would merely raise her T-shirt; instead she pulled it off entirely and lifted one arm. I stared at her. I had seen her in a bikini before—indeed, I had seen her topless—but as she sat on my futon in her bra I felt I had never seen her so naked. Her body had lost its tan and appeared almost blue in the glow of the television, and she was even more fit than I had remembered. She seemed otherworldly; she could have sprung from the pages of a graphic novel. I commanded myself to focus on her bruise; it was dark and angry at the top of her rib cage, bisected by the strap of her bra.

Without thinking, I extended my hand. Then I hesitated. She returned my gaze watchfully, but her expression did not change, so I touched her, placing my fingers on her bruise. She rested her hand on the back of her head as I traced the line of her ribs. I felt her skin break out in goose bumps, and I pulled her to me, embracing her gently and giving first her forehead, and then her lips, a kiss. She did not respond; she did not resist; she merely acceded as I undressed her. At times I would feel her hold onto me, or I would hear from her the faintest of gasps. Mainly she was silent and unmoving, but such was my desire that I overlooked the growing wound this inflicted on my pride and continued. I found it difficult to enter her; it was as though she was not aroused. She said nothing while I was inside her, but I could see her discomfort, and so I forced myself to stop.

"I'm sorry," she said. "No, I am sorry," I said. "You do not like it?" "I don't know," she said, and for the first time in my presence, her eyes filled with tears. "I just can't get wet. I don't know what's wrong with me." I held her in my arms, and as we lay there, she told me I was the first man she had been with since Chris—indeed, *other* than Chris. Her sexuality, she said, had been mostly dormant since his death. She had only once achieved orgasm, and that, too, by fantasizing of him. I did not know what to say. I wanted to console her, to accompany her into her mind and allow her to be less alone. So I asked her to tell me about him, how they had come to kiss, how they had come to make love. "You really want to know?" she asked. I replied that I did, and so she told me.

I knew bits and pieces of their story from before; that night I received it whole. Something of it seemed familiar to me; later I would realize what seemed familiar was the *emotion* with which she spoke, an emotion similar to that which she evoked in me. I attempted to separate myself from the situation, to listen to her as though I were not both aching for her and hurt that—seemingly despite herself—her body had rejected me. I succeeded in this to an extent that surprises me still, when I think of it today. Their story remains vivid in my mind, but I will not recount it now. Suffice it to say that theirs had been an unusual love, with such a degree of commingling of identities that when Chris died, Erica felt she had lost herself; even now, she said, she did not know if she could be found.

But as she spoke of him, her voice seemed to strengthen, and I felt her naked body soften and relax beside me. A liveliness entered her eyes; they ceased to be turned inward. She asked me about *my* experiences, about the nature of sex and relationships for teenagers in Pakistan. I told her I had had next to nothing in the way of sex before coming to America, and my relationships hardly amounted to much in the face of what she had just recounted. But they were delightful in their own way, I said, and I entertained her with anecdotes of Lahore for what seemed like hours. At one point I found myself gazing up at the ceiling as though I were gazing at the stars, and the two of us started to laugh. I felt we were at last becoming comfortable in the same bed, and as the sky outside began to lighten, I was compelled to stifle a good-natured yawn. She, too, was drowsy, she said, adding that I was better than any medication at putting her at ease. We fell asleep like that, not in one another's arms, but shoulder to shoulder, with our knuckles touching at our sides. Perhaps because of our conversation I dreamed not of Erica, but of home; what she dreamed of I did not know ...

But I observe, sir, that you are watching me with a rather peculiar expression. Possibly you find me crass for revealing such intimacies to you, a stranger? No? I will interpret that movement of your head as a response in the negative. Allow me to assure you that I do not always speak this openly; indeed, I almost never do. But tonight, as I think we both understand, is a night of some *importance*. Certainly I perceive it to be so—and yet if I am wrong, you will surely be justified in regarding me the most terrible boor!

7

I wonder now, sir, whether I believed at all in the firmness of the foundations of the new life I was attempting to construct for myself in New York. Certainly I *wanted* to believe; at least I wanted not to disbelieve with such an intensity that I prevented myself as much as was possible from making the obvious connection between the crumbling of the world around me and the impending destruction of my personal American dream. The power of my blinders shocks me, looking back—so stark in retrospect were the portents of coming disaster in the news, on the streets, and in the state of the woman with whom I had become enamored.

America was gripped by a growing and self-righteous rage in those weeks of September and October as I cavorted about with Erica; the mighty host I had expected of your country was duly raised and dispatched—but homeward, towards my family in Pakistan. When I spoke to them on the telephone, my mother was frightened, my brother was angry, and my father was stoical—this would all pass, he said. I found reassurance in my father's views, and I dressed myself in them as though they were my own. "Are you worried, man?" Wainwright asked me one day in the Underwood Samson cafeteria, resting his hand on my shoulder in a gesture of concern as I filled a bagel with smoked salmon and cream cheese. No, I explained, Pakistan had pledged its support to the United States, the Taliban's threats of retaliation were meaningless, my family would be just fine.

I ignored as best I could the rumors I overheard at the Pak-Punjab Deli: Pakistani cabdrivers were being beaten to within an inch of their lives; the FBI was raiding mosques, shops, and even people's houses; Muslim men were disappearing, perhaps into shadowy detention centers for questioning or worse. I reasoned that these stories were mostly untrue; the few with some basis in fact were almost certainly being exaggerated; and besides, those rare cases of abuse that regrettably did transpire were unlikely ever to affect me because such things invariably happened, in America as in all countries, to the hapless poor, not to Princeton graduates earning eighty thousand dollars a year.

Thus clad in my armor of denial I was able to focus—with continuing and noteworthy success—on my job. After the exceptional review I received for my performance in the Philippines, I had become Jim's fair-haired boy. He offered me another assignment on one of his teams, this time valuing an ailing cable operator. The firm was based in New Jersey—to which I began a daily commute—and had been hit hard by the decline in investor sentiment surrounding the technology sector in general and small-scale broadband providers in particular; it was barely able to service its debts and had become a prime candidate for acquisition.

On this occasion, our client was unconcerned with the potential for future growth. No, our mandate was to determine how much fat could be cut. Call centers, it was evident, could be outsourced; truck rolls could be reduced; purchasing could be consolidated with our client's existing operations. The potential for headcount reduction was substantial—and hence the reception our team received from the employees of the company was frosty indeed. Our telephone extensions and fax machines would mysteriously stop working; our security badges and notebooks would disappear. Often I would emerge into the car park to find that one of the tires of my rental car was punctured—far too often for it to be mere coincidence.

Once this happened when Jim had come out for the day; he had asked me to give him a ride back to the city. He shook his head as I brought out the spare. "Don't let it get you down, Changez," he said. "Time only moves in one direction. Remember that. Things always change." He loosened the metal strap of his watch, a solid, diver's chronometer, and let it slide to his knuckles. "When I was in college," he went on, "the economy was in bad shape. It was the seventies. Stagflation. But you could just smell the opportunity. America was shifting from manufacturing to services, a huge shift, bigger than anything we'd ever seen. My father had lived and died making things with his hands, so I knew from up close that that time was past." He refastened the clasp of his watch. Then he made a fist and twisted his thick forearm from side to side, slowly, until the instrument found its level. There was an almost ritualistic quality to his movements, like a batsman—or even, I would say, a knight—donning his gloves before striding onto a field of contest.

"The economy's an animal," Jim continued. "It evolves. First it needed muscle. Now all the blood it could spare was rushing to its brain. That's where I wanted to be. In finance. In the coordination business. And that's where *you* are. You're blood brought from some part of the body that the species doesn't need anymore. The tailbone. Like me. We came from places that were wasting away." I had finished replacing the tire, so I shut the boot and unlocked the doors. "Most people don't recognize that, kid," he said, buckling himself in beside me and nodding his head in the direction of the darkened building we had left. "They try to resist change. Power comes from *becoming* change."

I considered what Jim had said—both that evening, on the drive to Manhattan, and in the weeks that followed. There was a certain ring of truth to his words, but I was uncomfortable with the idea that the place I came from was condemned to atrophy. So I dwelled instead on the positive aspect of his little sermon: on the idea that I had chosen a field of endeavor that would be of ever-greater importance to humanity and would be likely, therefore, to provide me with ever-increasing returns. I also found myself better equipped to regard as misguided—or at least myopic—the resentment which seethed around us as we went about our business that autumn in that New Jersey corporate park.

But it would not be true to say I was completely untroubled. There were older people among the workers of the cable company. I sometimes sat near them in the cafeteria—although never at the same table; the seats beside our team always went untaken—and I imagined many of them had children my age. If English had a respectful form of the word *you*—as we do in Urdu—I would have used it to address them without the slightest hesitation. As it was, the nature of our interactions left me with minimal scope to show them deference—or even sympathy. I remarked upon this to Wainwright on one of the many weekend nights we found ourselves spending at the office, and he said, "You're working for the *man*, buddy. Didn't anyone tell you that at orientation?" Then he gave me a tired smile and added, "But I get where you're coming from. Just remember your deals would go ahead whether you worked on them or not. And focus on the fundamentals."

Focus on the fundamentals. This was Underwood Samson's guiding principle, drilled into us since our first day at work. It mandated a single-minded attention to financial detail, teasing out the true nature of those drivers that determine an asset's value. And that was precisely what I continued to do, more often than not with both skill and enthusiasm. Because to be perfectly honest, sir, the compassionate pangs I felt for soon-to-be-redundant workers were not overwhelming in their frequency; our job required a degree of commitment that left one with rather limited time for such distractions.

But then, in the latter part of October, something happened that upset my equanimity. It was shortly after Erica and I had abortively attempted to make love—perhaps a day or two later, although I can no longer precisely recall. The bombing of Afghanistan had already been under way for a fortnight, and I had been avoiding the evening news, preferring not to watch the partisan and sports-event-like coverage given to the mismatch between the American bombers with their twenty-first-century weaponry and the ill-equipped and ill-fed Afghan tribesmen below. On those rare occasions when I did find myself confronted by such programming—in a bar, say, or at the entrance to the cable company's offices—I was reminded of the film *Terminator,* but with the roles reversed so that the machines were cast as heroes.

What left me shaken, however, occurred when I turned on the television myself. I had reached home from New Jersey after midnight and was flipping through the channels, looking for a soothing sitcom, when I chanced upon a newscast with ghostly night-vision images of American troops dropping into Afghanistan for what was described as a daring raid on a Taliban command post. My reaction caught me by surprise; Afghanistan was Pakistan's neighbor, our friend, and a fellow Muslim nation besides, and the sight of what I took to be the beginning of its invasion by your countrymen caused me to tremble with fury. I had to sit down to calm myself, and I remember polishing off a third of a bottle of whiskey before I was able to fall asleep.

The next morning I was, for the first time, late for work. I had overslept and woken with a cracking headache. My fury had ebbed, but much though I wished to pretend I had imagined it entirely, I was no longer capable of so thorough a self-deception. I did, however, tell myself that I had overreacted, that there was nothing I could do, and that all these world events were playing out on a stage of no relevance to my personal life. But I remained aware of the embers glowing within me, and that day I found it difficult to concentrate on the pursuit—at which I was normally so capable—of fundamentals.

But listen! Did you hear that, sir, a muffled growl, as if of a young lion held captive in a gunnysack? That was my stomach protesting at going unfed. Let us now order our dinner. You would rather wait, you say, and eat upon your return to your hotel? But I insist! You must not pass up such an authentic introduction to Lahori cuisine; it will, given the dishes for which this market is justifiably renowned, be a purely carnivorous feast—one that harks back to an era before man's knowledge of cholesterol made him fearful of his prey—and all the more delectable for it.

Perhaps because we currently lack wealth, power, or even sporting glory—the occasional brilliance of our temperamental cricket team notwithstanding—commensurate with our status as the world's sixth most populous country, we Pakistanis tend to take an inordinate pride in our food. Here in Old Anarkali that pride is visible in the purity of the fare on offer; not one of these worthy restaurateurs would consider placing a western dish on his menu. No, we are surrounded instead by the kebab of mutton, the tikka of chicken, the stewed foot of goat, the spiced brain of sheep! These, sir, are *predatory* delicacies, delicacies imbued with a hint of luxury, of wanton abandon. Not for us the vegetarian recipes one finds across the border to the east, nor the sanitized, sterilized, processed meats so common in your homeland! Here we are not squeamish when it comes to facing the consequences of our desire.

For we were not always burdened by debt, dependent on foreign aid and handouts; in the stories we tell of ourselves we were not the crazed and destitute radicals you see on your television channels but rather saints and poets and—yes—conquering kings. *We* built the Royal Mosque and the Shalimar Gardens in this city, and *we* built the Lahore Fort with its mighty walls and wide ramp for our battle-elephants. And we did these things when your country was still a collection of thirteen small colonies, gnawing away at the edge of a continent.

But once more I am raising my voice, and making you rather uncomfortable besides. I apologize; it was not my intention to be rude. In any case, I ought instead to be explaining to you why I did not speak to Erica of my fury at seeing American troops enter Afghanistan. After that night when we celebrated in my bed her obtaining an agent, I had no contact with Erica for several days; she did not answer when I rang and she did not respond to my messages. I was hurt by this behavior—taking her silence for inconsideration—and I arrived in a reproachful mood for the drink that she eventually did invite me to. I was utterly unprepared for what I saw.

At the counter was a diminished Erica, not the

vivid, confident woman I knew but a pale, nervous creature who could almost have been a stranger. She seemed to have lost weight and her eyes darted about the bar. It was not until she smiled that something of the old Erica glimmered within her, but her smile left her face as quickly as it had come. My consternation must have been evident because she smiled again and said, "Do I look that bad?" "Not at all," I lied, "just tired, perhaps. Have you been unwell?" "Yeah," she said. "I'm sorry I didn't get back to you sooner." "That is quite all right," I said. "I hope I was not a pest." "Never," she said. "I've been going through a bad patch. It's happened before. But it hasn't been like this since the first time, after Chris died."

We ordered, beer for myself and a bottle of water for her, and I considered giving her an embrace but decided against it; she seemed too brittle to be touched. "What happens is," she went on, "my mind starts to go in circles, thinking and thinking, and then I can't sleep. And once a couple of days go by, if you haven't slept, you start to get sick. You can't eat. You start to cry. It just feeds on itself. I've got some stronger stuff from the doctor, so I've been sleeping again. But it isn't real sleep. And the rest of the day I feel like I'm out of it. Like when you get off a plane and you can't hear properly. Like that, except it's not just my hearing, and I can't pop my ears." She took a sip of her water and managed to wink at me. Then she said, "Freaky, huh?"

I stood there in silence, unable to think of what to say or even to offer her a smile; I was horrified. But she was waiting for me to respond, so I said, "But what is it you think of that causes you to become so upset?" "I think of Chris a lot," she said, "and I think of me. I think of my book. I think some pretty dark thoughts, sometimes. And I think of you." "What do you think of," I asked, "when you think of me?" "I think it isn't good for you to see me so much right now," she answered. "I mean it isn't good for you." "No," I reassured her, although I was frightened, "I want to see you." "That's what I mean," she said, looking into my eyes with great seriousness. "Do you get it? That's what I mean."

I did not get it in the least, and I asked her to come home with me. "I don't think I should," she said. "Really." But there was a softness in her expression, and when I continued to insist, she finally did acquiesce. During our taxi ride my mind struggled to comprehend what was happening. I had over these past weeks—sentimental and old-fashioned as it may sound, but then I was raised in a family where brief courtships were the norm—been indulging in daydreams of a life as Erica's husband; now I found not just those daydreams but the woman herself vanishing before my eyes. I wanted to help her, to hold onto her—indeed, I wanted to hold onto *us*—and I was desperate to extricate her from the maze of her psychosis. But I did not know how to proceed.

In my bed she asked me to put my arms around her, and I did so, speaking quietly in her ear. I knew she enjoyed my stories of Pakistan, so I rambled on about my family and Lahore. When I tried to kiss her, she did not move her lips or shut her eyes. So I shut them for her and asked, "Are you missing Chris?" She nodded, and I saw tears begin to force themselves between her lashes. "Then pretend," I said, "pretend I am him." I do not know why I said it; I felt overcome and it seemed, suddenly, a possible way forward. "What?" she said, but she did not open her eyes. "Pretend I am him," I said again. And slowly, in darkness and in silence, we did.

I do not know how to describe my experience of what happened next; I cannot, of course, claim that I was *possessed,* but at the same time I did not seem to be myself. It was as though we were under a spell, transported to a world where I was Chris and she was with Chris, and we made love with a physical intimacy that Erica and I had never enjoyed. Her body denied mine no longer; I watched her shut eyes, and her shut eyes watched *him.*

I can still recall her muscularity, made more pronounced by her gauntness, and the near-inanimate smoothness and coolness of her flesh as she leaned back and exposed to my touch her breasts. The entrance between her legs was wet and dilated, but was at the same time oddly rigid; it reminded me— unwillingly—of a wound, giving our sex a violent undertone despite the gentleness with which I attempted to move. More than once I smelled what I thought to be blood, but when I reached down to ascertain with my fingers whether it was her time of month, I found them unstained. She shuddered towards the end—grievously, almost mortally; her shuddering called forth my own.

"You're a kind person," she said afterwards, as we lay there. "It sounds like a stupid thing to say but it's true." I held her and did not reply. I felt something I have not felt before or since; I remember it well: I felt at once both *satiated* and *ashamed*. My satiation was understandable to me; my shame was more confusing. Perhaps, by taking on the persona of another, I had diminished myself in my own eyes; perhaps I was humiliated by the continuing dominance, in the strange romantic triangle of which I found myself a part, of my dead rival; perhaps I was worried that I had acted selfishly and I sensed, even then, that I had done Erica some terrible harm. But this last explanation is—I hope—unlikely; surely I could not have known what would happen to her over the weeks and months to follow.

Erica fell asleep that night without medication; I remained awake, in part because I had not yet eaten. I hesitated to rise and go to the refrigerator for fear of disturbing her, but her sleep was deep, like that of a child, and eventually I managed. I ate only bread and drank only water, a tasteless meal, but I kept at it until my belly was full, and when I returned to the bed it was as though I had a tight drum strapped to my front, which forced me to lie on my side.

It is impossible to tell, sir, given the gloom about us and the unexpressive cast of your face, but I suspect you are looking at me with a degree of revulsion; certainly I would look at you in such a manner if *you* had just told me what I have told you. But I hope your disgust has not banished your appetite, for I am summoning our waiter to take our order. Tonight, I can assure you, our meal will be anything but tasteless—and here he comes. Good man!

8

I observe, sir, that there continues to be something about our waiter that puts you ill at ease. I will admit that he is an intimidating chap, larger even than you are. But the hardness of his weathered face can readily be accounted for: he hails from our mountainous northwest, where life is far from easy. And if you should sense that he has taken a disliking to you, I would ask you to be so kind as to ignore it; his tribe merely spans both sides of our border with neighboring Afghanistan, and has suffered during offensives conducted by your countrymen.

Is he praying, you ask? No, sir, not at all! His recitation—rhythmic, formulaic, from memory, and so, I will concede, not unlike a prayer—is in actuality an attempt to transmit orally our menu, much as in your country one is told the specials. Here, of course, there are no specials; the excellent establishment of which tonight we are patrons has in all likelihood prepared precisely the same dishes for many years. I could translate for you but perhaps it would be better if I selected a number of delicacies for us to share. You will grant me that honor? Thank you. There, it is done, and off he goes.

I had been telling you of my disquiet on the night I finally made love to Erica—a night that ought, were ours a more normal relationship, to have been one of great joy. She left before dawn, waking with a start and insisting that she return home despite my requests that she stay. Once again, considerable time would pass before I heard from her again; my calls went unanswered, my messages unreturned. I had learned my lesson, and I desisted from attempting to make contact. But once a fortnight had gone by, I tried again and was rewarded by a response. She apologized, as she had previously done, for disappearing in this fashion; she said she thought it best, perhaps for her but certainly also for me, that we try not to see each other too often; and she consented to my request that we meet. "But come over to my place," she said. "I don't feel up to going out."

I was greeted at the door to Erica's apartment by

her mother, who ushered me into an antechamber
—which featured, among its antique decorations, a
bonsai tree and a harpsichord—and said, "I think
we need to chat. Erica has told you about her
history, yes?" I nodded. "Well," she went on, "her
condition has come back. It's serious. What she
needs right now is stability. No emotional up-
heavals, you get me? I can see you're a nice young
man. And I know she cares about you. But you
have to understand that she's a sick girl at the
moment. She doesn't need a boyfriend. She needs a
friend." She looked at me beseechingly. "I understand, madam," I said. "I will do whatever you
think best for her." "Thank you," she said. Then
she smiled and added, "It's easy to tell why she
likes you."

That conversation had a considerable impact on
me, not so much for what was said—although I was
alarmed by this grave characterization of Erica's
situation—but for *how* it was said; Erica's mother's
tone was one of quiet desperation, and it frightened
me. I entered Erica's room tentatively, attempting to
steel myself against what I might find. What I found
was not at first particularly alarming: Erica reclined

on her bed, pale, yes, as though she had a fever, and with hair that had gone some time since it was last washed, but seemingly in good spirits. She patted the space beside her and offered me her forehead to kiss as I sat down.

We spoke for a while as though nothing unusual had happened and we were meeting under the most ordinary of circumstances. I told her about my project in New Jersey—the negative reaction to our presence by the employees of the cable company, Jim's words of advice—and about the day-to-day occurrences in my life since she had seen me last. She told me about her doctor and her medication, how the drugs made it difficult to concentrate and so her days seemed to slip away with nothing to show for them. Given the relaxed manner in which she described it an observer would have been forgiven for thinking that her condition was not serious and she was on the mend—until I asked about her novel.

I immediately regretted doing so. Her eyes began to wander, and her voice became less sure. "I can't seem to work on it," she said. "Every time I try, I just get upset. I haven't been taking my agent's calls.

Poor guy. He must think I'm a lunatic." I remarked that writers were known to be eccentric and so it was unlikely her agent was particularly perturbed, and then I tried to change the subject, but she would not have it. "It doesn't help anymore," she said. "I used to turn to it, my writing, when I needed to get something out that was stuck inside. But I can't get it out now. It pulls me in, you know? I dwell on it instead of writing it." I tried to prevent myself from asking her what *it* was—whether because I thought it would upset her or because I thought it would upset me, I do not now know— but I failed. "It's whether there's something left," she explained, suddenly and unsettlingly calm, "or whether it's all already happened."

How can I describe to you, sir, how much her words disturbed me? She glanced away, and I saw her recede into her mind. I placed my hand next to hers, hoping as I had done innumerable times in the past to lure her out of her thoughts. I watched our skin—mine healthy and brown, hers sickly white— separated by a distance not greater than the width of an engagement ring, but she did not notice me. I waited for my proximity to make itself felt to her;

a minute passed in this fashion. Then she removed her hand from where it lay and—without ever looking in my direction—covered it with her other hand on her lap.

When Erica's mother entered shortly thereafter, I did not feel she was interrupting. No, she was not preventing the continuation of a discussion between her daughter and myself; she was merely bringing to an end my intrusion on a conversation Erica was having with Chris—a conversation occurring on some plane that I could not reach or even properly see. Erica waved a good-bye to me as I left her room, but she did so with her face averted, so I could not meet her gaze. Her mother thanked me for coming and asked me to wait for Erica to contact me before coming again. And with that, and a gentle kiss on the cheek, the door to the elevator was shut upon me and I began to travel down the shaft, alone.

I returned to my apartment and spent that night in semidarkness, in the glow of the city's lights entering through my windows, wondering as I would wonder for many months thereafter—indeed, as I sometimes wonder to this day—where

Erica was going. I never came to know what triggered her decline—was it the trauma of the attack on her city? the act of sending out her book in search of publication? the echoes raised in her by our lovemaking? all of these things? none of them?—but I think I knew even then that she was disappearing into a powerful *nostalgia,* one from which only she could choose whether or not to return.

For it was clear Erica needed something that I—even by consenting to play the part of a man not myself—was unable to give her. In all likelihood she longed for her adolescence with Chris, for a time before his cancer made her aware of impermanence and mortality. Perhaps the reality of their time together was as wonderful as she had, on more than one occasion, described to me. Or perhaps theirs was a past all the more potent for its being imaginary. I did not know whether I believed in the truth of their love; it was, after all, a religion that would not accept me as a convert. But I knew that *she* believed in it, and I felt small for being able to offer her nothing of comparable splendor instead.

I did not see Erica again that year. Thanksgiving

soon gave way to the chill of December, and every week—every day—I thought of calling her but prevented myself from doing so. Her mother had, of course, asked me to resist, and I suspect I thought, given the catastrophic progress of our relationship thus far, that imposing myself on her interior struggle would only do her harm. But I must admit that my motives were not entirely noble; there were in me at least some elements of the anger and hurt vanity that characterize a spurned lover, and these unworthy sentiments helped me to keep my distance. Still, I remained concerned for Erica's well-being—and remained also in the grip of a certain, probably irrational, *hope*—so the ongoing task of abstaining from communication was a struggle not unlike that of a man attempting to rid himself of an addiction.

Possibly this was due to my state of mind, but it seemed to me that America, too, was increasingly giving itself over to a dangerous nostalgia at that time. There was something undeniably retro about the flags and uniforms, about generals addressing cameras in war rooms and newspaper headlines featuring such words as *duty* and *honor*. I had always thought of America as a nation that looked forward; for the first time I was struck by its determination to look *back*. Living in New York was suddenly like living in a film about the Second World War; I, a foreigner, found myself staring out at a set that ought to be viewed not in Technicolor but in grainy black and white. What your fellow countrymen longed for was unclear to me—a time of unquestioned dominance? of safety? of moral certainty? I did not know—but that they were scrambling to don the costumes of another era was apparent. I felt treacherous for wondering whether that era was fictitious, and whether—if it could indeed be animated—it contained a part written for someone like me.

But what is that? Ah, your unusual telephone, beeping a demand for your attention. No, sir, I do not mind in the least; please proceed to key in your reply. It occurs to me that you have been contacted with the precision of an old church bell tower, by which I mean precisely on the hour—perhaps the company is checking up on you? No, you need not answer. But now that your response has been sent, allow me to direct your gaze to that grill where at this very moment our boneless chicken pieces are being set to roast. Observe the sparks that fly from the coals, angry and red, as our cook fans the flames. It is quite a beautiful sight, you must admit, and with it will soon come—*there,* do you smell it?—the most mouth-watering of aromas.

I had been telling you of the nostalgia that was becoming so prevalent in my world at the onset of the final winter I would spend in your country. But one notable bulwark continued to hold firm against this sentiment: Underwood Samson, which occupied most of my waking hours, and which was—as an institution—not nostalgic whatsoever. At work we went about the task of shaping the future with little regard for the past, and my personal efficacy continued to grow as I immersed myself in my project at the cable company, hoping, in this way, to leave behind the many worries that preyed upon me when I was free to ruminate.

I suspect I was never better at the pursuit of fundamentals than I was at that time, analyzing data as though my life depended on it. Our creed was one which valued above all else maximum productivity, and such a creed was for me doubly reassuring

because it was quantifiable—and hence *knowable*—
in a period of great uncertainty, and because it
remained utterly convinced of the possibility of
progress while others longed for a sort of *classical*
period that had come and gone, if it had ever existed
at all. I detected a change in my attitude to my
colleagues, a greater understanding of what drove
them to focus so completely on their professional
lives, and perhaps as a consequence it seemed for
a while that my popularity at the office was on
the rise.

Yet even at Underwood Samson I could not
entirely escape the growing importance of *tribe*.
Once I was walking to my rental car in the parking
lot of the cable company when I was approached
by a man I did not know. He made a series of un-
intelligible noises— *"akhala-malakhala,"* perhaps, or
"khalapal-khalapala"—and pressed his face alarm-
ingly close to mine. I shifted my stance, presenting
him with my side and raising my hands to shoulder
height; I thought he might be mad, or drunk; I
thought also that he might be a mugger, and I prepared to defend myself or to strike. Just then another
man appeared; he, too, glared at me, but he took his

friend by the arm and tugged at him, saying it was not worth it. Reluctantly, the first allowed himself to be led away. "Fucking Arab," he said.

I am not, of course, an Arab. Nor am I, by nature, a gratuitously belligerent chap. But my blood throbbed in my temples, and I called out, "Say it to my face, coward, not as you run and hide." He stopped where he was. I unlocked the boot, retrieving the tire iron from where it lay; the cold metal of its shaft rested hungrily in my hands, and I felt, at that moment, fully capable of wielding it with sufficient violence to shatter the bones of his skull. We stood still for a few murderous seconds; then my antagonist was once again pulled at, and he departed muttering a string of obscenities. When I sat in my car my hands were unsteady; I have, in the uniforms of the various teams for which I have played, had my share of fights—but this encounter had an intensity that was for me unprecedented, and it was some minutes before I deemed myself fit to drive.

What did he look like, you ask? Well, sir, he . . . But how odd! I cannot now recall the man's particulars, his age, say, or his build; to be honest, I cannot now recall many of the details of the events I have been relating to you. But surely it is the *gist* that matters; I am, after all, telling you a history, and in history, as I suspect you—an American—will agree, it is the thrust of one's narrative that counts, not the accuracy of one's details. Still, I can assure you that everything I have told you thus far happened, for all intents and purposes, more or less as I have described.

In any case, let us not allow ourselves to be diverted. Some days after the incident in the parking lot—close to the end of our project at the cable company—I was again driving back to Manhattan with Jim. It was late, and we were both hungry; he suggested, as I was dropping him off, that he panfry us a pair of tuna steaks. His flat was not the conservative, Upper East Side, liveried-doorman sort of place one might have expected; it was instead in TriBeCa, a four-thousand-square-foot loft that occupied the top floor of a nondescript building on Duane Street. Entering for the first time, I was struck by its *fashionable* quality, the sense it conveyed of attaching great value to design. Not that it was cluttered, or indeed feminine in any way; no, if anything it was a minimalist affair with cement floors and pipes conspicuously fastened to the ceiling. But each piece of furniture seemed perfectly curated—lit and positioned just so—and the walls featured impressive and forceful works of art, including, I realized, a not insignificant number of male nudes.

Jim rolled up his sleeves and asked, over the sizzle of our fish, what was on my mind. I sat at a stool, separated from him by the bar of his open-plan kitchen, which served also as a surface for dining. "Nothing, really," I said. "Is your family not at home?" He turned to me—visibly amused—and said, "I'm not married." "Ah," I said, "no children?" "No children," he affirmed, "but you're dodging my question." "What do you mean?" I asked. "You haven't been yourself lately," he said. "You're preoccupied. Something's eating at you. If I had to guess, I'd say it's your Pakistani side. You're worried about what's going on in the world." "No, no," I said, shaking my head to dismiss any possibility that my loyalties could be so divided, "things at home are a little unsettled, but it will pass." He seemed unconvinced. "Is your family okay?" he asked. "Yes," I said, "thank you." "All right then," he said, "but as I've told you before, I know what it's like to be an outsider. If you ever want to talk, give me a shout."

I left Jim's flat hoping I had thrown him off the scent. Still, my apparent transparency was alarming; Jim was a particularly perceptive observer, but if my internal conflicts were evident to him, then perhaps they were evident to others as well. I had heard tales of the discrimination Muslims were beginning to experience in the business world—stories of rescinded job offers and groundless dismissals—and I did not wish to have my position at Underwood Samson compromised. Besides, I knew that our firm, like much of our industry, had seen a sharp downturn in activity levels following the September attacks, and Wainwright had shared with me a rumor that cutbacks were on their way.

Our project at the cable company went on to end well—in the sense that we identified substantial cost savings and our client was pleased by the thoroughness of our valuation—but I was a nervous young man on the day of my December review. As it turned out, I need not have been so concerned.

Two of the six analysts in my entering class—those ranked fifth and sixth—were indeed among the employees our firm let go. But I, Jim informed me, was once again ranked number one; I was, in fact, awarded a prorated bonus that, although not enormous by the standards of our profession, was still rather generous given the expectation of lean times ahead. It enabled me to pay off, in full, my outstanding student loans and put aside a few thousand as well. I should have been ecstatic, but earlier that week armed men had assaulted the Indian parliament, and instead of celebrating my good fortune, I was confronting the possibility that soon my country could be at war.

My mother told me not to come; my father said much the same. But with the help of a Seventh Avenue travel consolidator and my sudden ability to afford Business Plus class airfare on PIA, I found myself bound for Lahore at that time of year when New York shoppers busy themselves with the purchasing of last-minute presents and couples can be seen kissing on the streets as they drag beautiful little shrubs to their apartments for use as Christmas trees. I sat on the airplane next to a man who removed his shoes—much to my dismay—and who said, after praying in the aisle, that nuclear annihilation would not be avoided if it was God's will, but God's will in this matter was as yet unknown. He offered me a kindly smile, and I suspected that his purpose in making this remark was to reassure me.

And with that, sir, the moment has come for us to eat! For your own safety, I would suggest that you avoid this yoghurt and those chopped vegetables. What? No, no, I meant nothing sinister; your stomach might be upset by uncooked foods, that is all. If you insist, I will go so far as to sample each of these plates myself first, to reassure you that there is nothing to fear. Here. A piece of warm bread, like so—ah, fresh from the clay oven—and I will begin.

9

Will they provide us with cutlery, you ask? I am certain, sir, that a fork can be found for you, but allow me to suggest that the time has now come for us to dirty our hands. We have, after all, spent some hours in each other's company already; surely you can no longer feel the need to hold back. There is great satisfaction to be had in touching one's prey; indeed, millennia of evolution ensure that manipulating our meals with our skin heightens our sense of taste—and our appetite, for that matter! I see you need no further convincing; your fingers are tearing the flesh of that kebab with considerable determination.

There are adjustments one must make if one comes here from America; a different way of *observing* is required. I recall the Americanness of my own gaze when I returned to Lahore that winter when war was in the offing. I was struck at first by how shabby our house appeared, with cracks running through its ceilings and dry bubbles of paint flaking off where dampness had entered its walls. The electricity had gone that afternoon, giving the place a gloomy air, but even in the dim light of the hissing gas heaters our furniture appeared dated and in urgent need of reupholstery and repair. I was saddened to find it in such a state—no, more than saddened, I was shamed. *This* was where I came from, this was my provenance, and it smacked of lowliness.

But as I reacclimatized and my surroundings once again became familiar, it occurred to me that the house had not changed in my absence. *I* had changed; I was looking about me with the eyes of a foreigner, and not just any foreigner, but that particular type of entitled and unsympathetic American who so annoyed me when I encountered him in the classrooms and workplaces of your country's elite. This realization angered me; staring at my reflection in the speckled glass of my bathroom mirror I resolved to exorcize the unwelcome sensibility by which I had become possessed.

It was only after so doing that I saw my house

properly again, appreciating its enduring grandeur, its unmistakable personality and idiosyncratic charm. Mughal miniatures and ancient carpets graced its reception rooms; an excellent library abutted its veranda. It was far from impoverished; indeed, it was rich with history. I wondered how I could ever have been so ungenerous—and so blind—to have thought otherwise, and I was disturbed by what this implied about myself: that I was a man lacking in substance and hence easily influenced by even a short sojourn in the company of others.

But far more significant than these inward-oriented musings of mine was the external reality of the threat facing my home. My brother had come to collect me from the airport; he embraced me with sufficient force to cause my rib cage to flex. As he drove he ruffled my hair with his hand. I felt suddenly very young—or perhaps I felt my age: an almost childlike twenty-two, rather than that permanent middle-age that attaches itself to the man who lives alone and supports himself by wearing a suit in a city not of his birth. It had been some time since I had been touched so easily, so familiarly, and I smiled. "How are things?" I asked him. He shrugged. "There is an artillery battery dug in at the country house of a friend of mine, half an hour from here, and a colonel billeted in his spare bedroom," he replied, "so things are not good."

My parents seemed well; they were more frail than when I had seen them last, but at their age that was to be expected with the passage of a year. My mother twirled a hundred-rupee note around my head to bless my return; later it would be given to charity. My father's eyes glistened, moist and brown. "Contact lenses," he said, dabbing them with a handkerchief, "quite smart, eh?" I said they suited him, and they did; his glasses had come late in life, and they had concealed the strength of his face. Neither he nor my mother wanted to discuss the possibility of war; they insisted on feeding me and hearing in detail about my life in New York and my progress at my new job. It was odd to speak of that world here, as it would be odd to sing in a mosque; what is natural in one place can seem unnatural in another, and some concepts travel rather poorly, if at all. I censored any mention of Erica, for example, and indeed of anything that I thought might disturb them.

But that night a family banquet was held in my honor, and there the conflict with India dominated conversation. Opinion was divided as to whether the men who had attacked the Indian parliament had anything to do with Pakistan, but there was unanimity in the belief that India would do all it could to harm us, and that despite the assistance we had given America in Afghanistan, America would not fight at our side. Already, the Indian army was mobilizing, and Pakistan had begun to respond: convoys of trucks, I was told, were passing through the city, bearing supplies to our troops on the border; as we ate, we could hear the sounds of military helicopters flying low overhead; a rumor circulated that soon traffic would be halted on the motorway so that our fighter planes could practice landing on it, in case all of our airfields were destroyed in a nuclear exchange.

It will perhaps be odd for you—coming, as you do, from a country that has not fought a war on its own soil in living memory, the rare sneak attack or terrorist outrage excepted—to imagine residing within commuting distance of a million or so hostile troops who could, at any moment, attempt a full-scale invasion. My brother cleaned his shotgun. One of my uncles stocked up on bottled water and canned food. Our part-time gardener was deployed with the reserves. But for the most part, people seemed to go about their lives normally; Lahore was the last major city in a contiguous swath of Muslim lands stretching west as far as Morocco and had therefore that quality of understated bravado characteristic of frontier towns.

But I worried. I felt powerless; I was angry at our weakness, at our vulnerability to intimidation of this sort from our—admittedly much larger—neighbor to the east. Yes, we had nuclear weapons, and yes, our soldiers would not back down, but we were being threatened nonetheless, and there was nothing I could do about it but lie in my bed, unable to sleep. Indeed, I would soon be gone, leaving my family and my home behind, and this made me a kind of coward in my own eyes, a traitor. What sort of man abandons his people in such circumstances? And what was I abandoning them for? A well-paying job and a woman whom I longed for but who refused even to see me? I grappled with these questions again and again.

When the time came for me to return to New York I told my parents I wanted to stay longer, but they would not hear of it. Perhaps they sensed that I was myself divided, that something called me back to America; perhaps they were simply protecting their son. "Do not forget to shave before you go," my mother said to me. "Why?" I asked, indicating my father and brother. "They have beards." "They," she replied, "have them only because they wish to hide the fact that they are bald. Besides, you are still a boy." She stroked my stubble with her fingers and added, "It makes you look like a mouse."

On the flight I noticed how many of my fellow passengers were similar to me in age: college students and young professionals, heading back after the holidays. I found it ironic; children and the elderly were meant to be sent away from impending battles, but in our case it was the fittest and brightest who were leaving, those who in the past would have been most expected to remain. I was filled with contempt for myself, such contempt that I could not bring myself to converse or to eat. I shut my eyes and waited, and the hours took from me the responsibility even to flee.

You are not unfamiliar with the anxieties that precede armed conflict, you say? Aha! Then you have been in the service, sir, just as I suspected! Would you not agree that waiting for what is to come is the most difficult part? Yes, quite so, not as difficult as the time of carnage itself—said, sir, like a true soldier. But I see that you have paused in your eating; perhaps you are waiting for fresh bread. Here, have half of mine. No, I insist; our waiter will bring us more momentarily.

Given your background, you will doubtless have experienced the peculiar phenomenon that is the return to an environment more or less at peace from one where the prospect of large-scale bloodshed is a distinct possibility. It is an odd transition. My colleagues greeted with considerable—although often partially suppressed—consternation my reappearance in our offices. For despite my mother's request, and my knowledge of the difficulties it could well present me at immigration, I had not shaved my two-week-old beard. It was, perhaps, a form of protest on my part, a symbol of my identity, or perhaps I sought to remind myself of the reality I had just left behind; I do not now recall my precise motivations. I know only that I did not wish to blend in with the army of clean-shaven youngsters who were my coworkers, and that inside me, for multiple reasons, I was deeply angry.

It is remarkable, given its physical insignificance—it is only a hairstyle, after all—the impact a beard worn by a man of my complexion has on your fellow countrymen. More than once, traveling on the subway—where I had always had the feeling of seamlessly blending in—I was subjected to verbal abuse by complete strangers, and at Underwood Samson I seemed to become overnight a subject of whispers and stares. Wainwright tried to offer me some friendly advice. "Look, man," he said, "I don't know what's up with the beard, but I don't think it's making you Mister Popular around here." "They are common where I come from," I told him. "Jerk chicken is common where I come from," he replied, "but I don't smear it all over my face. You need to be careful. This whole corporate collegiality veneer only goes so deep. Believe me."

I appreciated my friend's concern, but I did not take his suggestion. Despite the layoffs, the utilization rate at our firm remained low in January, and I sat at my desk with little to do. I spent this time online, reading about the ongoing deterioration of affairs between India and Pakistan, the assessment by experts of the military balance in the region and likely scenarios for battle, and the negative impact the standoff was already beginning to have on the economies of both nations. I wondered how it was that America was able to wreak such havoc in the world—orchestrating an entire war in Afghanistan, say, and legitimizing through its actions the invasion of weaker states by more powerful ones, which India was now proposing to do to Pakistan—with so few apparent consequences at home.

I also, after six weeks of attempting not to communicate with her, finally called Erica, and because her phone was constantly off, followed up by sending an email. I would like to claim my message was brief, a polite hello that was for the most part respectful of her request for silence, but in truth I spent many hours composing it and it was perhaps the lengthiest I have ever written. In it I told her of what had been happening in my life, both at work and at home, and the turmoil through which I was passing; I also told her how much I missed her and that I did not understand where or why she had gone. It was some days before she replied. "I'm at a sort of clinic," she wrote, "an institution where people can recover themselves. I think of you, too." She invited me to come and visit her; it would be easier for her to attempt to answer my questions face-to-face.

The clinic was an afternoon's drive from the city, a converted villa set in fifty acres of secluded countryside overlooking the Hudson River. I was greeted by a nurse in the reception area. "You must be Changez," she said. "Erica has told me a lot about you." "I am," I said. "How did you know?" "Eyelashes like a Maybelline ad," she replied, "that's what she said." As I considered this unlikely description, the nurse explained that Erica had been waiting for me but became a little nervous and went for a walk, asking the nurse to explain a few things on her behalf. "So she will not see me?" I asked. The nurse smiled. "Sure she will, honey," she said, "but people get embarrassed sometimes when they're in a place like this. She thinks it won't be as awkward for you both if I talk to you first." She patted my hand. Then she added, "I'm like the shower you take before you jump into a swimming pool."

What I had to understand about Erica, the nurse told me, was that she was in love with someone else. She knew it would be tough for me to hear, but I had to hear it regardless. It did not matter that the person Erica was in love with was what the nurse or I might call deceased; for Erica he was alive enough, and that was the problem: it was difficult for Erica to be out in the world, living the way the nurse or I might, when in her mind she was experiencing things that were stronger and more meaningful than the things she could experience with the rest of us. So Erica felt better in a place like this, separated from the rest of us, where people could live in their minds without feeling bad about it. "But eventually she will have to leave here," I said. "Perhaps she will want to be with me then." The nurse shook her head. "Maybe," she said, "but right now you're the hardest person for her to see. You're the one who upsets her most. Because you're the most real, and you make her lose her balance."

The nurse suggested I was likely to find Erica at the end of a path that wound through the wooded grounds, in a small copse on a hilltop. She was indeed there, sitting on a bench of rough-hewn timber. She wore a heavy jacket and turned at my approach; she was gaunt, her flesh seeming almost bruised where it passed over the bones of her face, and she glowed with something not unlike the fervor of the *devout*. She extended her hand, but instead of shaking it I kissed it, my lips touching the synthetic polymers of her winter glove. She smiled. "You look cute," she said. "Your beard brings out your eyes." I thought she looked like someone who was about to complete the month of fasting and had been too consumed by prayer and reading of the holy book to give sufficient thought to the nightly meal, but I did not say so.

She offered me her arm and we strolled together, speaking softly; the mist of our breathing preceded us. "This is a good place for me right now," she said. "I feel calm here." "You seem calm," I said, resisting the urge to add, *too calm*. "I'm sorry I've been hiding," she said. "It's not that I haven't wanted to see you. It's just that I could see I was pulling you in, and I didn't want you to get hurt. I thought it would be better for you like this." "Why would I get hurt?" I asked. "It hurts when you care about someone and they go away," she replied. "But where are you going?" I asked. She shrugged and did not answer.

We walked on in silence but for the sound of snow crunching under our feet; my ears began to ache from the cold. "Do you write here?" I asked. "No," she said, "not in the sense of putting stuff down. But I think a lot. I imagine." "And do I sometimes figure in your imaginings?" I asked. "Sometimes," she said, smiling. "Any fantasies of kinky sex," I said, "with an exotic foreigner given to role-playing?" She laughed and squeezed my arm; for the first time her face seemed to soften, to become almost vulnerable. But then she again receded inside herself. "You helped me," she said. "You were kind and true, and I'm grateful."

It was the certainty with which she placed me in the past tense that struck me most about her statement. I felt hope being quenched within me, and although I said, "Do not be grateful, be lust-ful—come back to New York with me," I said it without that core of conviction that gives words their power; she leaned her head momentarily against my shoulder, but she was not compelled to respond. I watched her out of the corner of my eye as we made our way to the main building together, wondering how much of her detached and seemingly ascetic state was a consequence of the medication she was consuming. For a moment, I was seized by the wild notion of abducting her and taking her away with me in my rental car; surely my ministrations would be more productive in restoring her to reality than the chemicals she was subjecting herself to here. But the absurdity—and disrespect to her—of such an act was immediately obvious to me, and I did nothing of the sort.

"Do you know how to ski?" she asked me. "No," I said, "I have never been." "Chris and I," she said, "used to go every winter—Colorado, usually, or once in a while Vermont. We even did a little cross-country together in Central Park, when we were kids. We each got a pair as a present and we snuck out with them without telling anyone.

We got into trouble. Our parents called the police. It was fun, though. Anyway, this place reminds me of that. Especially the snow on that slope. It's so gentle and it seems so soft. You should go sometime." We had reached the gravel of the driveway. "You should take me," I said. She shook her head. "I can't," she said, "but you should still go. Try to be happy, okay? I'm sorry about everything. Please take care of yourself."

She gave me a hug and afterwards she stood there, looking at me. But he is *dead*, I wanted to shout! It was all I could do not to kiss her then; perhaps I should have. I had to choose whether to continue to try to win her over or to accept her wishes and leave, and in the end I chose the latter. Maybe, I told myself as I drove away, it was a test and I failed; maybe I should have risked it. I almost turned around and went back, but in the end I did not do so. Things might have worked out rather differently if I had turned around; then again, things might have worked out exactly the same.

I cut a desolate figure in the office after that, angry and preoccupied with thoughts of Erica and of home. I was negligent at my administrative duties, and did absolutely nothing to seek out a new assignment for myself. I half expected someone to come to my desk with a pink slip to put me out of my misery. Instead, Jim summoned me to issue a surprising stamp of approval. "Listen, kid," he said, "some people around here think you're looking kind of shabby. The beard and all. Quite frankly, I don't give a shit. Your performance is what counts, as far as I'm concerned, and you're the best analyst in your class by a long way. Besides, I know it must be tough for you with what's going on in Pakistan. What you need is to get yourself busy, which I'll admit isn't easy when we have as dry a pipeline as we do right now. But I've got a new project, valuing a book publisher in Valparaiso, Chile. It's going to have to be a small team, just a vice president and an analyst. Normally, I'd offer it to someone with more experience. But I'm offering it to you. What do you think?" "Thank you, sir," I muttered. He laughed. "A bit of enthusiasm, please," he said, adding, "It's a lot of responsibility. There won't be any backup for you." "You can rely on me," I said, this time with what I hoped was greater apparent sincerity. I do not know if I succeeded, however, because although Jim smiled in response, his expression was one of puzzlement.

But I observe that you, sir, have stopped eating. Can it be that you are full? Very well, I will not insist; I will, however, order us some dessert, a little rice pudding with sliced almonds and cardamom, the perfect sweetener for an evening such as ours, which is taking a turn towards the grimmer side. Such dishes may not normally be to your taste, but I would encourage you to have, at the very least, a tiny bite. After all, one reads that the soldiers of your country are sent to battle with chocolate in their rations, so the prospect of sugaring your tongue before undertaking even the bloodiest of tasks cannot be entirely alien to you.

When you sit in that fashion, sir, with your arm curved around the back of the empty chair beside you, a bulge manifests itself through the lightweight fabric of your suit, precisely at that point parallel to the sternum where the undercover security agents of our country—and indeed, one assumes, of all countries—tend to favor wearing an armpit holster for their sidearm. No, no, please do not adjust your position on my account! I did not mean to imply that you were so equipped; I am certain that in your case it is merely the outline of one of those travel wallets in which the prudent secrete their possessions so that they are less likely to be discovered by thieves.

I myself employed no such precautions on my trip to Chile. We again flew in the relative comfort of first class, but I was no longer excited by the luxuries of our cabin; unlike Jim, who was as usual accompanying us for the commencement of the project, and the vice president who would be my immediate commanding officer for the full duration of this tour, I turned down our flight attendant's many offers of champagne. For all the hours that we were airborne, I neither ate nor slept; my thoughts were caught up in the affairs of continents other than the one below us, and more than once I regretted coming at all.

I wondered what I could do to help Erica. Seeing her as I had seen her last—emaciated, detached, and so lacking in *life*—pained me; I recalled the dog we had had in my childhood and his passivity and desire for solitude in those last days before he succumbed to the leukemia induced in him by that brand of tick powder a veterinarian would subsequently tell us never to use. But Erica was not suffering from leukemia; there was no physical reason for her malaise beyond, perhaps, a biochemical disposition towards mental disorders of this kind. No, hers was an illness of the spirit, and I had been raised in an environment too thoroughly permeated with a tradition of shared rituals of mysticism to accept that conditions of the spirit could not be influenced by the care, affection, and desire of others. What was essential was that I seek to understand why I had failed to penetrate the membrane with which she guarded her psyche; my more direct approaches had been rejected, but with sufficient insight I might yet be welcomed through a process of osmosis. I could imagine no alternative but to try; my longing for her was undiminished despite our months of near-complete separation.

It was in such a frame of mind that I arrived in Santiago. We traveled from there by road—making good progress except for a brief blockage where the mechanical shovels of repair crews tore out great bites of the red earth that characterizes Chile's central valley—and we smelled our destination before we saw it; Valparaiso lay on the briny Pacific and was hidden from view by a crest of hills.

The chief of the publishing company was an old man by the name of Juan-Bautista, given to smoking unfiltered cigarettes and sporting glasses thick enough to burn through paper on a sunny day. He reminded me of my maternal grandfather; I liked him at once. "What do you know of books?" he asked us. "I specialize in the media industry," Jim replied. "I've valued a dozen publishers over two decades." "That is finance," Juan-Bautista retorted. "I asked what you knew of books." "My father's uncle was a poet," I found myself saying. "He was well-known in the Punjab. Books are loved in my family." Juan-Bautista looked at me as though becoming aware of the presence of this youngster before him for the first time; I did not speak in that meeting again.

Jim explained to us afterwards that Juan-Bautista was not pleased to have us there. Although he had run the company for many years, he did not own it; the owners wanted to sell, and the prospective buyer—our client—was unlikely to continue to subsidize the loss-making trade division with income from the profitable educational and professional publishing arms. Trade, with its stable of literary—defined for all practical purposes as commercially unviable—authors was a drag on the rest of the enterprise; our task was to determine the value of the asset if that drag were shut down.

We set ourselves up in a handsome, if aging, conference room with a large oval table and bookshelves lining the walls. When a strong breeze blew,

I could hear outside our windows the clicking of wooden storm shutters against their restraints. It was hot during the afternoons—we had come during the southern summer—but sometimes we would wake to fog and a morning chill, and in those moments I was glad for the wool of my suit. Jim left after two days, remarking in my presence to the vice president that he could expect impressive things of me. But although my laptop was open, my Internet connection enabled, and my pen and notebook positioned by my side—I found myself unable to concentrate on our work.

Instead I perused news websites which informed me that Pakistan and India were conducting tit-for-tat tests of their ballistic missiles and that a stream of foreign dignitaries was visiting the capitals of both countries, urging Delhi to desist from its warlike rhetoric and Islamabad to make concessions that would enable a retreat from the brink of catastrophe. I wondered, sir, about your country's role in all this: surely, with American bases already established in Pakistan for the conduct of the Afghanistan campaign, all America would have to do would be to inform India that an attack on

Pakistan would be treated as an attack on any American ally and would be responded to by the overwhelming force of America's military. Yet your country was signally failing to do this; indeed, America was maintaining a strict neutrality between the two potential combatants, a position that favored, of course, the larger and—at that moment in history—the more belligerent of them.

These thoughts preoccupied me when I should have been gathering data and building my financial model. Moreover, Valparaiso was itself a distraction: the city was powerfully atmospheric; a sense of melancholy pervaded its boulevards and hillsides. I read online about its history and discovered that it had been in decline for over a century; once a great port fought over by rivals because of its status as the last stop for vessels making their way from the Pacific to the Atlantic, it had been bypassed and rendered peripheral by the Panama Canal. In this— Valparaiso's former aspirations to grandeur—I was reminded of Lahore and of that saying, so evocative in our language: *the ruins proclaim the building was beautiful*.

I sensed the vice president was growing

increasingly irritated with me; I could hardly blame him: he was working from morning until midnight, poor fellow, with little support from his only teammate. I pretended to be keeping myself busy, but as the days passed and my deadlines began to slip, he lost patience. "Look, man," he said, "what's the problem? You're not getting anything done. I know you're supposed to be good, but from my perspective, you aren't delivering squat. Tell me what you need. You want help with your model, more direction? Tell me and I'll give it to you, but for God's sake pull it together." He was a manager of excellent repute, and I might have considered revealing to him the turmoil taking place inside me, but at the level of human beings our connection was nil. So I apologized, saying that his feedback had hit the mark, but that he need not worry because I would redouble my efforts. "Everything," I said, mustering a tone of maximum reassurance, "is under control."

For a time this appeared to satisfy him, although it was patently untrue. Yet I knew he had begun to resent me—and rightly so, after all: by not performing to plan I was making him look bad—and for my part I was beginning to resent him as well. I could not respect how he functioned so completely immersed in the structures of his professional micro-universe. Yes, I too had previously derived comfort from my firm's exhortations to focus intensely on work, but now I saw that in this constant striving to realize a financial future, no thought was given to the critical personal and political issues that affect one's emotional present. In other words, my blinders were coming off, and I was dazzled and rendered immobile by the sudden broadening of my arc of vision.

I noticed Juan-Bautista watching me as I shuffled about half-heartedly from one meeting to another. He kept his door open and his desk was positioned in such a way that it was possible for him to gaze down the corridor. Once, as I was passing by, he called me to him. "I have," he said, "looked into this matter of the contemporary poets of the Punjab. Tell me, what was the name of your father's uncle?" I told him and he nodded; he had indeed seen him mentioned in an anthology available in Spanish translation. I was surprised and pleased to hear that this was the case, but before I could respond he

went on to say, "You seem very unlike your colleagues. You appear somewhat lost." "Not at all,"
I replied, taken aback. Then I added, "Although I
must say I am quite moved by Valparaiso." He
suggested that I visit the house of Pablo Neruda,
but to go during the day as it was shut in the
evening, and with that our brief conversation
concluded.

I never came to know why Juan-Bautista singled
me out. Perhaps he was gifted with remarkable
powers of empathy and had observed in me a
dilemma that out of compassion he thought he
could help me resolve; perhaps he saw among his
enemies one who was weak and could easily be
brought down; perhaps it was mere coincidence.
Sentimentally, I would like to believe in the
first of these possibilities. But regardless, Juan-
Bautista added considerable momentum to my
inflective journey, a journey that continues to this
day . . .

But I am getting ahead of myself, and in any case
our dessert has arrived. He has brought only a single
bowl; I sensed that you were not keen on having
more than a taste, and the same is true of myself,

as I am now quite full. What do you think, sir? Ah, that puckering of your lips is an inauspicious sign. Too sweet, you say? An interesting observation, given that I have always felt your country to be rather similar to mine in the intensity of its national desire for sweetness. But perhaps you are atypical; your travels have taken you far from the ubiquitous soda fountains and ice-cream bars of your motherland.

I too had traveled far that January, but the home of Neruda did not feel as removed from Lahore as it actually was; geographically, of course, it was perhaps as remote a place as could be found on the planet, but in spirit it seemed only an imaginary caravan ride away from my city, or a sail by night down the Ravi and Indus. I told the vice president that I was going out to inspect a distribution center and with this excuse made my way up into the hills, climbing higher and higher, until when I turned to look at the ocean I saw gulls soaring at the same altitude as myself. The neighborhood was a poor one, with colorful murals like graffiti on the walls and children racing by on wooden carts that appeared to be shipping crates to which wheels had been attached. The house itself was compact and beautiful, reminiscent of a boat jutting out over the bay; a garden cascaded below it, and behind the bar was a convex mirror, which Neruda had employed to convince his guests that they were drunk. I lingered on the terrace and watched the sun dip lower in the sky. In the distance, someone was playing the guitar; it was a delicate melody, a song with no words.

I thought of Erica. It occurred to me that my attempts to communicate with her might have failed in part because I did not know where I stood on so many issues of consequence; I lacked a stable *core*. I was not certain where I belonged—in New York, in Lahore, in both, in neither—and for this reason, when she reached out to me for help, I had nothing of substance to give her. Probably this was why I had been willing to try to take on the persona of Chris, because my own identity was so fragile. But in so doing—and by being unable to offer her an alternative to the chronic nostalgia inside her— I might have pushed Erica deeper into her own confusion. I resolved to write this to her in an email, as a sort of apology, perhaps, and as an invitation to resume the contact between us that she had all but severed, and I recall pressing send without rereading even once what I had written.

But days passed without any response, and I began to lose hope that one would come. I telephoned my parents and they told me that the situation in Pakistan continued to be precarious; it was rumored that India was acting with America's connivance, both countries seeking through the threat of force to coerce our government into changing its policies. Moreover, our house's main water connection had ruptured—the pipes were long overdue for replacement—and the pressure was now so low that it had become impossible to take a shower; they were making do with buckets and ladles instead. This caused me to reflect again on the absurdity of my situation, being two hemispheres—if such a thing is possible—from home at a time when my family was in need.

The only manner in which I could be of aid to them at that moment was to provide money, and this I did, wiring what little savings I possessed to my brother because my father refused to accept it. The act of calling my bank to arrange the transfer ought to have impressed upon me the importance of my job: after all, I had no other source of income to fall back on. But instead my indifference to my work continued unabated. There was no longer any possibility of deceiving the vice president; my lapses had become obvious, and his reprimands grew increasingly blunt. I wonder in retrospect why he did not reach out to Jim at that stage to have me replaced, but then again, this was not entirely surprising: the task of a vice president at our firm— the word vice in the title notwithstanding—was to be as close to autonomous as possible. A good vice president was one who *got things done,* no matter what, and to appeal for assistance prematurely would be to undermine one's superior's confidence in one's abilities.

As for myself, I was clearly on the threshold of great change; only the final catalyst was now required, and in my case that catalyst took the form of lunch. Juan-Bautista's invitation caught me off guard; he simply mentioned, as I was passing his office one day, that it would be a shame to have visited Valparaiso without having tasted sea bass cooked in salt, and as he intended to go to his favorite restaurant that afternoon, I really ought—if I were free—to accompany him. I said—out of politeness and curiosity, and also because I was eager to seize any pretext to avoid returning to the poisonous atmosphere of our team room—that it would be an honor, and the next thing I knew, I found myself making my way through the streets of the city with a man who desired more than any other to see our client's acquisition fail to proceed.

Juan-Bautista wore a hat and carried a walking stick, and he ambled at a pace so slow that it would likely have been illegal for him to cross at an intersection in New York. When we were seated and he had ordered on our behalf, he said, "I have been observing you, and I think it is no exaggeration to say, young man, that you seem upset. May I ask you a rather personal question?" "Certainly," I said. "Does it trouble you," he inquired, "to make your living by disrupting the lives of others?" "We just value," I replied. "We do not decide whether to buy or to sell, or indeed what happens to a company after we have valued it." He nodded; he lit a cigarette and took a sip from his glass of wine. Then he asked, "Have you heard of the janissaries?"

"No," I said. "They were Christian boys," he explained, "captured by the Ottomans and trained to be soldiers in a Muslim army, at that time the greatest army in the world. They were ferocious and utterly loyal: they had fought to erase their own civilizations, so they had nothing else to turn to."

He tipped the ash of his cigarette onto a plate. "How old were you when you went to America?" he asked. "I went for college," I said. "I was eighteen." "Ah, much older," he said. "The janissaries were always taken in childhood. It would have been far more difficult to devote themselves to their adopted empire, you see, if they had memories they could not forget." He smiled and speculated no further on the subject. Our food arrived shortly thereafter and the sea bass may well have been as splendid as he had claimed; unfortunately, I can no longer recall its taste.

But your expression, sir, tells me that you think something is amiss. Did this conversation really happen, you ask? For that matter, did this so-called Juan-Bautista even exist? I assure you, sir: you can trust me. I am not in the habit of inventing untruths! And moreover, even if I were, there is no reason why this incident would be more likely to be false than any of the others I have related to you. Come, come, I believe we have passed through too much together to begin to raise questions of this nature at so late a stage.

In any case, Juan-Bautista's words plunged me into a deep bout of introspection. I spent that night considering what I had become. There really could be no doubt: I was a modern-day janissary, a servant of the American empire at a time when it was invading a country with a kinship to mine and was perhaps even colluding to ensure that my own country faced the threat of war. Of course I was struggling! Of course I felt torn! I had thrown in my lot with the men of Underwood Samson, with the officers of the empire, when all along I was predisposed to feel compassion for those, like Juan-Bautista, whose lives the empire thought nothing of overturning for its own gain.

In the morning, with the demeanor of a man facing a firing squad—no, that is perhaps too dramatic, and a dangerous comparison on this of all evenings, but you understand my intent—I told the vice president that I refused to work any further. He was baffled. "What do you mean, refuse?" he said. "I am done here," I replied. "I intend to return to New York." Panic ensued; a conference call with Jim was hastily arranged. "Look, kid," an uncharacteristically tense Jim said over the speakerphone, "I know you have stuff on your mind. But if you walk out on this now you undermine our firm. You hurt your team. In wartime soldiers don't really fight for their flags, Changez. They fight for their friends, their buddies. Their team. Well, right now your team is asking you to stay. Afterwards, if you need a break, it's yours."

I must admit, Jim's words gave me pause. I had great admiration for him; he had always stood by me, and now I proposed to betray him. By the time my replacement could be dispatched and brought up to speed, it was probable that the deadline for our valuation would be missed. Jim had sent me as an act of faith and generosity; my repayment would be a slap in the face and all the more impudent for coming at a time of financial weakness for the firm. Besides, without my job—which I was certain to lose—my visa would expire, and I would be compelled to leave the United States. But I resolved not to consider such things at that moment; I did not want to wonder whether I was abandoning any hope of being with Erica. All I knew was that my days of focusing on fundamentals were done. And so, the following evening, two weeks ahead of schedule, I boarded a flight bound for New York.

Ah, our waiter approaches with green tea, the perfect aid to digestion after a heavy meal. Remarkable service, eh? He has arrived just as he was required. One would not have thought, sir, that he was watching us so closely, but the night is now well advanced, and there are no longer any other customers to divert his attention.

11

It is odd how the character of a public space changes when it is empty; the abandoned amusement park, the shuttered opera house, the vacant hotel: in films these often feature as backdrops for events intended to frighten. So it is with this market: now that our fellow visitors have dwindled in number to a sporadic and scattered few, it has taken on a rather more ominous edge. Perhaps it has to do with the cloudy sky above, through which one occasionally glimpses a gash of moon, or perhaps it is the darkening shadows in the warren of alleyways slipping away from here in all directions, but I would suggest that it is instead our *solitude* that most disturbs us, the fact that we are all but alone despite being in the heart of a city. Ah! There, sir, do you smell it: the aroma of dust on that warm breeze? That is the smell of the desert to the south, a smell that, were we to encounter it in your homeland, would in all likelihood foreshadow the passage through this dimly lit stage of a desolate ball of tumbleweed.

Although the atmosphere that surrounded me on my flight from Santiago to New York was precisely the opposite—the cabin was bright and close to full—my thoughts belonged to a setting like that which you and I occupy at this moment. Yes, my musings were bleak indeed. I reflected that I had always resented the manner in which America conducted itself in the world; your country's constant interference in the affairs of others was insufferable. Vietnam, Korea, the straits of Taiwan, the Middle East, and now Afghanistan: in each of the major conflicts and standoffs that ringed my mother continent of Asia, America played a central role. Moreover I knew from my experience as a Pakistani—of alternating periods of American aid and sanctions—that finance was a primary means by which the American empire exercised its power. It was right for me to refuse to participate any longer in facilitating this project of domination; the only surprise was that I had required so much time to arrive at my decision.

I resolved to look about me with an ex-janissary's

gaze—with, that is to say, the analytical eyes of a product of Princeton and Underwood Samson, but unconstrained by the academic's and the professional's various compulsions to focus primarily on parts, and free therefore to consider also the *whole* of your society—upon my return to New York. Seen in this fashion I was struck by how traditional your empire appeared. Armed sentries manned the check post at which I sought entry; being of a suspect race I was quarantined and subjected to additional inspection; once admitted I hired a charioteer who belonged to a serf class lacking the requisite permissions to abide legally and forced therefore to accept work at lower pay; I myself was a form of indentured servant whose right to remain was dependent upon the continued benevolence of my employer. *Thank you, Juan-Bautista,* I thought as I lay myself down in my bed, *for helping me to push back the veil behind which all this had been concealed!*

But I must have been in a peculiar emotional state, in a sort of semi-hypnotic daze, for when I woke in the morning my feelings were entirely different. It was then that I was hit by the enormity of what I was giving up. Where else could I—

without money and family contacts, and at so young an age—hope to attain such an impressive income? Would I not miss this city of possibility, with its magical vibrancy and sense of excitement? What about my duty to Erica, or rather the duty to myself that was born of my desire for her? And how would I face Jim?

If you have ever, sir, been through the breakup of a romantic relationship that involved great love, you will perhaps understand what I experienced. There is in such situations usually a moment of passion during which the unthinkable is said; this is followed by a sense of euphoria at finally being liberated; the world seems fresh, as if seen for the first time; then comes the inevitable period of doubt, the desperate and doomed backpedaling of regret; and only later, once emotions have receded, is one able to view with equanimity the journey through which one has passed. My doubt and regret came rather quickly, as they so often—in my experience of our species— tend to do, and when I boarded the subway to report for duty at Underwood Samson for the last time, I was in a state of shock similar to that which one undergoes when one has witnessed one's knee twist impossibly but has yet to feel any pain.

Not—please understand me—that I was convinced that I had made a mistake; no, I was merely unconvinced that I had *not* made a mistake. I was, in other words, confused. Nevertheless, my pride compelled me to attempt to appear unaffected by the unexpected sadness within me. I did not permit my gaze to linger on the imposing reception area—which struck me now as reminiscent of the gleaming façade of some exalted and exclusive temple—or on the spectacular view from our windows; I did not permit myself to pocket a box of my business cards, elegantly printed proof that I had once been selected from among hundreds to be here. I simply let myself be led by the pair of security guards who stood on either side of me, watched as I placed a limited number of clearly personal possessions into a small cardboard box, and then escorted me to human resources for my exit conversation.

This was surprisingly brief—stern and dauntingly formal, but without recrimination—and once the requisite forms had been signed and data relevant to performance-enhancing indicators gathered, I was told that Jim wanted to speak with me. He was wearing a dark suit and a dark tie—funereal colors, I thought—and he looked under-slept. "You really screwed us, kid," he said. "I know," I replied. "I am sorry." "I'm not a big believer in compassion at the workplace," he went on. "I didn't think twice when it came to firing you. In fact, I wish I'd done it a month ago and saved us the headache you've given us down in Valparaiso. But," he paused, "I'll tell you this. I like you, Changez. I can see you're going through a crisis. If you ever need to get something off your chest and you want someone to talk to, call and I'll buy you a beer." My throat constricted; I could not reply. I nodded slowly, a gesture not unlike a bow.

After leaving Jim's office, I was marched to the elevator bank. I realized how deep was the suspicion I had engendered in my colleagues over these past few—bearded and resentful—weeks; only Wainwright came over to shake my hand and say farewell; the others, if they bothered to look at me at all, did so with evident unease and, in some cases, a fear which would not have been inappropriate had I been convicted of plotting to kill them rather than of abandoning my post in mid-assignment. The guards did not leave me until I was outside the building, and it was only then that I allowed myself to rub my eyes with the back of my hand, for they had been watering slightly.

You must remember that I was only twenty-two and this had been my first proper job; at such an age and in such a situation events have an emotional resonance that is perhaps exaggerated. In any case, I felt as though a world had ended—which, indeed, it had—and I made my way to the East Village on foot. I imagine I was a rather odd sight—a distraught and hirsute Pakistani carrying an unmarked box through the center of Manhattan—but I do not recall receiving any untoward comments from passersby; then again, I was in all likelihood too preoccupied to have noticed.

In my flat I poured myself a whiskey and sat thinking. It was still early—not yet midday—and so I decided to call my family. My brother answered. He had received the money I had sent, he said, and workers had already dug up and exposed our rotting pipes. By tomorrow they ought to have been replaced. I told him that I had decided to move back to Lahore. He attempted to dissuade me; tension with India was mounting. He had been recently to Islamabad, he said, and spouses and children of foreigners assigned to embassies and NGOs were leaving the country. I explained that I had no choice; "I got fired," I said, "and my visa will soon be invalid." He told me the family would of course look after me. I did not say that I had hoped to be the one looking after *them,* and I continued to cradle my drink for some time after the call was done.

But your own glass, sir, has now remained empty a good while. Shall I request our bill? A quick wave and yes, here he comes. How much, you ask? Please do not worry yourself; you are a guest here and this—it is only a tiny amount—is on me. You wish to pay half? Absolutely not; besides, here we pay all or we pay none. You have reminded me of how alien I found the concept of acquaintances splitting a bill when I first arrived in your country. I had been raised to favor mutual generosity over mathematical precision in such matters; given time both work equally well to even a score.

I had not, however, been schooled in the etiquette of how best to contact a lover who had retreated to a mental institution, and so I vacillated between emailing Erica and going to see her in person. In the end, my decision was made for me: I tried to email her but my message bounced back—with a notice saying it could not be delivered because her inbox was full—and so I rented a car and appeared at the facility unannounced. I was told at reception that visitors without invitations were not welcome—and in any case they could neither confirm nor deny if Erica was even there—but just as it seemed they were about to ask me to leave, I saw the nurse I had met on my previous trip and appealed to her to intervene on my behalf.

"I'll talk to him," she said to the receptionist, taking me aside. She looked flustered and suggested I sit down. "What do you know?" she asked me. "What do I know," I said, "about what?" "I'm so sorry," she said. "Erica's gone." I asked what precisely she meant, *gone,* and the nurse explained. Erica had vanished about two weeks ago, indeed shortly after I had seen her last. She had not liked to be alone when she had first come to the institution; she would spend hours with the nurses and the counselors and her fellow patients, and especially with the nurse with whom I was speaking. But towards the end of her stay she had increasingly been wandering off by herself, until one day she had walked out and not come back. Her clothes had been found on a rocky bluff overlooking the Hudson, neatly folded in a pile.

"Are you trying to tell me that she killed herself?" I said. "They haven't recovered any remains," the nurse said, "and she didn't leave a note. Technically she's a missing person. But she'd been saying goodbye to everyone." I asked if she could show me the place from which Erica might have jumped, and she led me through the grounds until we stood there. It was a beautiful spot to commit suicide, perhaps to run out from between the snow-dusted conifers, to push off from the granite and sail through the air, gazing across at the far bank of the mighty river, where a small house exhaled smoke from its chimney, before crashing into the icy current below. But I could not imagine Erica's pale, naked body following that arc.

So I drove back to the city and went immediately to her apartment. Erica's mother was not wearing any makeup; I noticed her eyebrows were so fine as to be almost nonexistent. I explained that I had just returned from the institution; had she heard from Erica? Her mother stared at me as though I had slapped her without provocation. "No," she said, recovering herself and speaking wearily, "I'm afraid not." "Please know," I said, "that I will do anything which is of assistance to you." "Thank you," she said, inviting me inside. She told me that the emergency services would remain on the lookout for Erica, and ongoing advertisements had been purchased in the local newspapers; beyond that there was little one could do. We attempted to speak of inconsequential matters, but this proved difficult—when she asked how I was, I said I had just been fired; when I asked the same, she could only muster a wan smile—and so we sat mainly in silence. But before I left, she did two things, I suspect out of kindness: first, she told me that Erica had mentioned that she had found me rather dashing in my new beard; and second, she gave me a copy of Erica's manuscript. "Maybe," her mother said, "you'd like to read it."

I did not do so for over a week; it sat undisturbed on top of my television. During that time I waited for a sign from Erica—an email, a phone call, a ring on my buzzer—but none ever came. I wandered about the city revisiting places she had taken me to, whether because I thought I might see her or because I thought I might see something of us, I am not now certain. A few of these places—such as the gallery in Chelsea we had visited on the night of our first date—I proved unable to find; they had vanished as though they had never existed. Others, like the spot in Central Park where we had gone on our picnic, were easy to locate but seemed to have altered. Perhaps this was the effect of a change in season; perhaps also it was in the city's nature to be inconstant.

I remembered Erica in September, at what was still the start of our relationship, just after the attacks on the World Trade Center. Although it is traditionally associated with the end of summer and the impending arrival of autumn, September has always seemed to me a month of beginnings, a *spring* of sorts—possibly because it marks the commencement of the academic year. I was diving into my life in New York in September, full of optimism at what was to come. One evening I was walking with Erica through Union Square and we saw a firefly.

"Look!" she said, amazed. "It's trying to compete with the buildings." Indeed it was: a tiny greenish glow visible up close but overwhelmed by the city's luminance when viewed from even a modest distance. We watched as it crossed Fourteenth Street, headed south. Erica stood in front of me, her back to my chest, and I placed my arms around her, resting my palms on her belly. It felt an intimate gesture—like that of an expectant father with his pregnant wife—and she leaned against me. I can still recall the movement of her muscles as she breathed. A taxi sped by and we lost sight of the firefly. "Do you think he made it?" she asked me. "I have no idea," I said, "but I hope so."

Such memories occupied my waking hours in those days after her disappearance, and likely also permeated my dreams; they were in that period my only form of contact with her. But eventually I did read the manuscript her mother had given me. I must admit, I was frightened to do so—as though it might be the last time I would hear Erica's voice— and I was nervous about what that voice might say. Yet her novel was no tortured, obviously auto- biographical affair. It was simply a tale of adventure, of a girl on an island who learns to make do. The narrative shimmered with hope, and although it was for the most part rather spare, it paused often to delight in little details: in the texture of the skin of a piece of fallen fruit, for example, or in the swaying antennae of crayfish in a stream.

I could not locate Erica in the rhythms or sounds of what she had written; it seemed a mistake, offered me no clues. It was so purposeful, so resolute in being precisely what it was that I was baffled. I was also powerfully affected. When I put down the manuscript, it was not with the conviction that Erica was either alive or dead. But I had begun to understand that she had chosen not to be part of my story; her own had proven too compelling, and she was—at that moment and in her own way—following it to its conclusion, passing through places I could not reach. I saw I had no option but to pursue my own preparations to leave.

I would like to claim that my final days in New York passed in a state of enlightened calm; nothing could be further from the truth. I was an incoherent and emotional madman, flying off into rages and sinking into depressions. Sometimes I would lie in bed, thinking in circles, asking the same questions about why and where Erica had gone; sometimes I would find myself walking the streets, flaunting my beard as a provocation, craving conflict with anyone foolhardy enough to antagonize me. Affronts were everywhere; the rhetoric emerging from your country at that moment in history—not just from the government, but from the media and supposedly critical journalists as well—provided a ready and constant fuel for my anger.

It seemed to me then—and to be honest, sir, seems to me still—that America was engaged only in posturing. As a society, you were unwilling to reflect upon the shared pain that united you with those who attacked you. You retreated into myths of your own difference, assumptions of your own superiority. And you acted out these beliefs on the stage of the world, so that the entire planet was rocked by the repercussions of your tantrums, not least my family, now facing war thousands of miles away. Such an America had to be stopped in the interests not only of the rest of humanity, but also in your own.

I resolved to do so, as best I could. But first I had

to depart. I rode to JFK on a crisp, clear afternoon, an afternoon that reminded me of my trip to the institution and the view from that bluff above the Hudson. I thought of Erica removing her clothes and then, having shed her past, walking through the forest until she met a kindly woman who took her in and fed her. I thought of how cold she would have been on that walk. And so I left my jacket on the curb as a sort of offering, as my last gesture before returning to Pakistan, a wish of warmth for Erica—not in the way one leaves flowers for the dead, but rather as one twirls rupees above the living. Later, through the windows of the terminal, I saw that I had caused a security alert, and I shook my head in exasperation.

What exactly did I do to stop America, you ask? Have you really no idea, sir? You hesitate—never fear, I am not so rude as to forcibly extract an answer. I will tell you what I did, although it was not much and I fear it may well fail to meet your expectations. But first let us leave this market; the shutters are coming down, and some unsavory characters are lurking about. Where are you staying? The Pearl Continental, you say? I will walk you.

No, it is not far, and although it is dark and parts of our route will at this time be deserted, we should be fine. Lahore is, as I have said before, quite safe from the standpoint of petty crime—and besides we are both fortunately possessed of those aspects of stature and appearance that tend to give ruffians pause.

12

From your backward glance, sir, I gather you have noticed that we were not alone in our desire to depart. Yes, others have made their way to Mall Road behind us, such as that waiter who was so unusually attentive and yet seemed to rub against your grain. There is nothing surprising in that; the evening's work is now done. I would ask you to direct your gaze instead to these lovely build-ings—in varying states of disrepair—which date to the British era and function geographically and architecturally as a link between the ancient and contemporary parts of our city. How delightful they are: a chemist, an optician, a purveyor of fine saris, a gentleman's tailor. Observe how often the words *brothers* and *sons* appear in their signage; these are family-run establishments, passed gently from generation to generation. No, not in the case of that retailer of guns and ammunition, as you correctly

194   MOHSIN HAMID

point out—but surely you must concede for the most part that they are charming and rather quaint.

These plazas are a different matter entirely, with their harsh outlines and cramped façades; they were built largely in the seventies and eighties, before the instinct of historical preservation began to take hold, and they mottle the surface of this area like an irritation of the skin. I find them particularly unpleasant at night, unlit and empty, bounded by those narrow passageways into which one could imagine being dragged against one's will, forever to disappear! Yes, you are quite right: let us quicken our pace; we have a fair distance yet to cover.

Are you familiar with *The Legend of Sleepy Hollow*? You have seen the film, you say? I have not, but I am sure it was faithful; certainly the prose version was a most powerful work. One cannot but join in the terror of poor Ichabod Crane, alone on his horse, in that moment when he first perceives the presence of the Headless Horseman. I must admit, I am sometimes reminded of the sound of those spectral clip-clops when I go for nocturnal walks by myself. How they make my heart pound! But clearly you do not share my pleasure at this thought;

indeed you appear decidedly anxious. Allow me, then, to change the subject . . .

I had been telling you earlier, sir, of how I *left* America. The truth of my experience complicates that seemingly simple assertion; I had returned to Pakistan, but my inhabitation of your country had not entirely ceased. I remained emotionally entwined with Erica, and I brought something of her with me to Lahore—or perhaps it would be more accurate to say that I lost something of myself to her that I was unable to relocate in the city of my birth. Regardless, the effect of this was to pull and tug at my moods; waves of mourning washed over me, sadness and regret prompted at times by an external stimulus, and at others by an internal cycle that was almost *tidal,* for want of a better word. I responded to the gravity of an invisible moon at my core, and I undertook journeys I had not expected to take.

Often, for example, I would rise at dawn without having slept an instant. During the preceding hours, Erica and I would have lived an entire day together. We would have woken in my bedroom and breakfasted with my parents; we would have dressed for work and caressed in the shower; we would have sat on our scooter and driven to campus, and I would have felt her helmet bumping against mine; we would have parted in the faculty parking area, and I would have been both amused and annoyed by the stares she received from the students passing by, because I would not have known how much those stares owed to her beauty and how much to her foreignness; we would have gone out for an inexpensive but delicious dinner in the open air, bathed by the moonlight beside the Royal Mosque; we would have spoken about work, about whether we were ready for children; I would have corrected her Urdu and she my course plan; and we would have made love in our bed to the hum of the ceiling fan.

I have also been transported in ways that were no less vivid but far more fleeting. I recall once, during the monsoon, watching a puddle form in the rut of a muddy tire track beside the road. As raindrops fell and water filled the banks of this little lake, I noticed a stone standing upright in the center, like an island, and I thought of the joy Erica would have had at gazing upon that scene. Similarly, I recall another incident, after I had a collision on my scooter, when I returned home and stripped off my shirt to see a livid bruise on my rib cage, where hers had once been. I stared at myself in the mirror and touched my skin with my fingers and hoped that the mark would not soon fade, as it inevitably did.

Such journeys have convinced me that it is not always possible to restore one's boundaries after they have been blurred and made permeable by a relationship: try as we might, we cannot reconstitute ourselves as the autonomous beings we previously imagined ourselves to be. Something of us is now outside, and something of the outside is now within us. Perhaps you have had no comparable experience, for you are gazing at me as though at a raving madman. I do not mean to say that we are all *one,* and indeed—as will soon become evident to you—I am not opposed to the building of walls to shield oneself from harm; I merely wished to explain certain aspects of my behavior upon my return.

Despite my not insubstantial financial constraints, I managed every year to pay my class dues in order to receive the *Princeton Alumni Weekly,* which I read unfailingly from cover to cover, with particular attention to the class notes and obituaries sections at the end. From time to time I would chance upon the name of an acquaintance and I would squint intently through such pinholes into the life I had left behind, wondering how that world—the world of people like those with whom I had traveled to Greece—was evolving. Erica, however, never appeared in those pages, and while it was possible that mention of her had slipped by unnoticed in one of the issues that the vagaries of the international post had prevented from arriving, I drew hope and sorrow in equal measure from each of her episodic absences.

I do not know what I expected to find—a notice that her novel had been published and she had thrilled classmates by appearing at the book launch? a final announcement that her body had been identified? a blurry face in a reunion photograph that could plausibly have been hers?—but I do know that time did not diminish the eagerness with which I looked. For some months I continued to email her, until her account became inactive; thereafter I limited myself to a single letter each year, sent on the anniversary of her disappearance, but it was always returned to me unopened.

My brother married last April, shortly before I turned twenty-five. Subsequently my mother began to suggest—with increasing urgency—that I consider doing the same; she believed I was in the grip of an unhealthy melancholy and that a family of my own was the surest way for me to rediscover satisfaction in my life. She also thought I spent too much time at work or alone in my room, and not enough with my friends. Once she even asked me with visible nervousness if I was not, by any chance, gay. I had not told her about Erica, and I found it became progressively more difficult to contemplate doing so; our relationship could now thrive only in my head, and to discuss it with a mother intent—admittedly in my own best interest—on challenging it with reality might do it irreparable harm. Not, of course, that I actually *believe* I am having a relationship, in the normal sense of that term, with Erica at this moment, or that she will one day appear, smiling and bent against the weight of her backpack, to surprise me on my doorstep. But I am still young and see no need to marry another, and for now I am content to wait.

You, sir, on the other hand, seem ready to bolt. What has so startled you? Was it that sound in the distance? I assure you, it was not the report of a pistol—although I can understand why you might think so—but rather the misfiring exhaust of a passing rickshaw. Their two-stroke motors, often not in the best of maintenance, are prone to sputtering in that fashion. It is most disturbing, I agree. What? Is somebody following us? I cannot see anyone—no, wait, now that you mention it there are a few figures there, in the gloom. Well, we cannot expect to have Mall Road to ourselves, even at this late hour. In all likelihood they are merely workers making their way home.

Yes, you are right: they have paused. What do you mean, sir, did I give them a signal? Of course not! I have as little insight into their motivations and identities as you do. One can only speculate that they have dropped something, or are engaged in conversation among themselves. Or perhaps they are wondering why *we* have paused, and whether we mean them ill! Regardless, there is no need for us to concern ourselves overmuch; let us continue with our midnight stroll. Lahore is a city of eight million people, after all; it is hardly a rural forest inhabited by phantoms.

I am glad you are willing to proceed. But what are you searching for? Ah, your unusual mobile phone. If you are sending a text to your colleagues, you may wish to inform them that we are not far from your hotel—another fifteen minutes at the most, I should think, which suggests to me that I ought to make haste if I am to bring matters to a suitable conclusion. Earlier, sir, if you recall, you asked me what I did to stop America. Let me now, as we come to the end of our time together, attempt an answer, even though it may well leave you disappointed.

The threat of war with India reached its highest point the summer after I returned from New York. Multinational corporations on both sides of the border ordered senior employees to leave, and travel advisories were issued throughout the nations of the First World, counseling their citizens to defer nonessential trips to our region. It seemed the weather was the only factor delaying the official commencement of hostilities: first because the heat was too great for an Indian offensive in the desert, then because the monsoon's rains made driving treacherous for Indian tanks in the Punjab. September was deemed the best month for battle, since the mountain passes of Kashmir might be closed by snow as early as October. So we waited as our September ticked by—little noticed by the media in your country, which was focused at that time on the first anniversary of the attacks on New York and Washington—and then the days started to shorten, the negotiations began to make progress, and the likelihood of a catastrophe that could have claimed tens of millions of lives receded. Of course, humanity's respite was brief: six months later the invasion of Iraq would be under way.

A common strand appeared to unite these conflicts, and that was the advancement of a small coterie's concept of American interests in the guise of the fight against terrorism, which was defined to refer only to the organized and politically motivated killing of civilians by killers *not* wearing the uniforms of soldiers. I recognized that if this was to be the single most important priority of our species, then the lives of those of us who lived in lands in which such killers also lived had no meaning except as collateral damage. This, I reasoned, was why America felt justified in bringing so many deaths to Afghanistan and Iraq, and why America felt justified in risking so many more deaths by tacitly using India to pressure Pakistan.

I had in the meanwhile gotten a job as a university lecturer, and I made it my mission on campus to advocate a disengagement from your country by mine. I was popular among my students—perhaps because I was young, or perhaps because they could see the practical value of my ex-janissary's skills, which I imparted to them in my courses on finance—and it was not difficult to persuade them of the merits of participating in demonstrations for greater independence in Pakistan's domestic and international affairs, demonstrations that the foreign press would later, when our gatherings grew to newsworthy size, come to label anti-American.

The first of our protests to receive much attention took place not far from where we are now. Your country's ambassador was in town, and we surrounded the building in which he was speaking, chanting and holding placards. There were thousands of us, of all possible affiliations—communists, capitalists, feminists, religious literalists—and things began to get out of hand. Effigies were burned and stones were thrown, and then we were charged at by large numbers of uniformed and plain-clothed police. Scuffles broke out, I intervened in one, and as a result I spent the night in prison, nursing a bloody lip and bruised knuckles.

My office hours were soon overrun by meetings with politically minded youths, so much so that I was often forced to stay on until after dinner to ensure that I had dealt satisfactorily with the curricular and extracurricular demands of all those who sought me out. Naturally, I became a mentor to many of these men and women: advising them not only on their papers and their rallies, but also on matters of the heart and a vast range of other topics—from drug rehabilitation and family planning to prisoners' rights and shelters for battered spouses.

I will not pretend to you that all of my students were angels; some, I will be the first to admit, were no better than common thugs. But over the years

I have developed the ability to take quick stock of a person—an ability that, I would be remiss not to point out, is in no small measure modeled on that of *my* former mentor, Jim—and while I will not claim to be infallible, I think it is fair to say that my sense of another's character is generally very good. I can usually tell, for example, who in a crowd is most likely to provoke violence, or who among my peers is most likely to complain to the dean that I need to be put in my place before my activities get out of hand.

I have received official warnings on more than one occasion, but such is the demand for my courses that I have until now escaped suspension. And lest you think that I am one of *those* instructors, in cahoots with young criminals who have no interest in education and who run their campus factions like marauding gangs, I should point out that the students I tend to attract are bright, idealistic scholars possessed of both civility and ambition. We call each other comrades—as, indeed, we do all those we consider like-minded—but I would not hesitate to use the term *well-wishers* instead. So it was with immense consternation that I learned recently that one of them had been arrested for planning to assassinate a coordinator of your country's effort to deliver development assistance to our rural poor.

I had no inside knowledge of this supposed plot—which was all the more perverse for its alleged targeting of an agent of compassion—but I was certain that the boy in question had been implicated by mistake. How could I be certain, you ask, if I had no inside knowledge? I must say, sir, you have adopted a decidedly unfriendly and accusatory tone. What precisely is it that you are trying to imply? I can assure you that I am a believer in nonviolence; the spilling of blood is abhorrent to me, save in self-defense. And how broadly do I define self-defense, you ask? Not broadly at all! I am no ally of killers; I am simply a university lecturer, nothing more nor less.

I see from your expression that you do not believe me. No matter, I am confident of the truth of my words. In any case, it was impossible to ask the boy himself about the matter, as he had disappeared—whisked away to a secret detention facility, no doubt, in some lawless limbo between your country and mine. He and I were not particularly well acquainted, as I have repeatedly testified, but I remembered his shy smile and aptitude for cash-flow statements, and I found myself filled with rage at the mystery surrounding his treatment. When the international television news networks came to our campus, I stated to them among other things that no country inflicts death so readily upon the inhabitants of other countries, frightens so many people so far away, as America. I was perhaps more forceful on this topic than I intended.

Later, it occurred to me that in addition to expressing my dismay, I was possibly trying to attract attention to myself; I had, in my own manner, issued a firefly's glow bright enough to transcend the boundaries of continents and civilizations. If Erica was watching—which rationally, I knew, she almost certainly was not—she might have seen me and been moved to correspond. I was tugged at by an undercurrent of loss when she did not do so. But my brief interview appeared to resonate: it was replayed for days, and even now an excerpt of it can be seen in the occasional war-on-terror montage. Such was its impact that I was warned by my comrades that America might react to my admittedly intemperate remarks by sending an emissary to intimidate me or worse.

Since then, I have felt rather like a Kurtz waiting for his Marlow. I have endeavored to live normally, as though nothing has changed, but I have been plagued by paranoia, by an intermittent sense that I am being observed. I even tried to vary my routines—the times I left for work, for example, and the streets I took—but I have come to realize that all this serves no purpose. I must meet my fate when it confronts me, and in the meantime I must conduct myself without panic.

Most of all, I must avoid doing what you are doing in this instant, namely constantly looking over my shoulder. It seems to me that you have ceased to listen to my chatter; perhaps you are convinced that I am an inveterate liar, or perhaps you are under the impression that we are being pursued. Really, sir, you would do well to relax. Yes, those men are now rather close, and yes, the expression on the face of that one—what a coincidence; it is our waiter; he has offered me a nod of recognition—is rather grim. But they mean you no harm, I assure you. It seems an obvious thing to say, but you should not imagine that we Pakistanis are all potential terrorists, just as we should not imagine that you Americans are all undercover assassins.

Ah, we are about to arrive at the gates of your hotel. It is here that you and I shall at last part company. Perhaps our waiter wants to say goodbye as well, for he is rapidly closing in. Yes, he is waving at me to detain you. I know you have found some of my views offensive; I hope you will not resist my attempt to shake you by the hand. But why are you reaching into your jacket, sir? I detect a glint of metal. Given that you and I are now bound by a certain shared intimacy, I trust it is from the holder of your business cards.

PENGUIN ESSENTIALS

Eva Luna by Isabel Allende

Lucky Jim by Kingsley Amis

Regeneration by Pat Barker

Out of Africa by Karen Blixen

An Ice-Cream War by William Boyd

Any Human Heart by William Boyd

A Start in Life by Anita Brookner

A Clockwork Orange by Anthony Burgess

Junky by William S. Burroughs

Breakfast at Tiffany's by Truman Capote

In Cold Blood by Truman Capote

A Month in the Country by J. L. Carr

The Big Sleep by Raymond Chandler

Heart of Darkness by Joseph Conrad

The Man in the High Castle by Philip K. Dick

My Family and Other Animals by Gerald Durrell

The Circle by Dave Eggers

Invisible Man by Ralph Ellison

The Great Gatsby by F. Scott Fitzgerald

Tender is the Night by F. Scott Fitzgerald

PENGUIN ESSENTIALS

A Room with a View by E.M. Forster

Cold Comfort Farm by Stella Gibbons

Goodbye to All That by Robert Graves

The Diary of a Nobody by George and Weedon Grossmith

The Reluctant Fundamentalist by Mohsin Hamid

The Thin Man by Dashiell Hammett

Steppenwolf by Hermann Hesse

I'm the King of the Castle by Susan Hill

High Fidelity by Nick Hornby

Three Men in a Boat by Jerome K. Jerome

Dubliners by James Joyce

On the Road by Jack Kerouac

Lady Chatterley's Lover by D.H. Lawrence

The Periodic Table by Primo Levi

A Short History of Tractors in Ukrainian by Marina Lewycka

The Road to Lichfield by Penelope Lively

Lolita by Vladimir Nabokov

Wide Sargasso Sea by Jean Rhys

Bonjour Tristesse by Françoise Sagan

White Teeth by Zadie Smith

PENGUIN ESSENTIALS

The Prime of Miss Jean Brodie by Muriel Spark

Are You Experienced? by William Sutcliffe

Hell's Angels by Hunter S. Thompson

A Confederacy of Dunces by John Kennedy Toole

Cat's Cradle by Kurt Vonnegut

A Handful of Dust by Evelyn Waugh

Brideshead Revisited by Evelyn Waugh

Twilight by Elie Wiesel

The Day of the Triffids by John Wyndham

Mrs Dalloway by Virginia Woolf

PENGUIN ESSENTIALS

ARE YOU EXPERIENCED?/WILLIAM SUTCLIFFE

'India does that to you . . .'

Liz has always wanted to travel in the Far East – to lose herself in a different world and make a spiritual connection with another culture. Dave has always wanted to get into Liz's pants. So they decide to go backpacking in India.

Liz loves it and is inspired by the other travelers she meets; Dave is horrified, and soon decides that anyone who enjoys backpacking must be crazy.

It's going to be a long three months . . .

'Spot on. A marvellously funny satire. Bull's eye' *Daily Telegraph*

HIGH FIDELITY/NICK HORNBY

'If you really wanted to mess me up, you should have got to me earlier . . .'

Rob and Laura have split up. But Rob isn't miserable. He's free. He can do what he wants when he wants: like listen to the music *he* likes, see other people, and show Laura that she never mattered *that* much. Except despite how hard he tries, Rob can't seem to move on. And when he sees Laura again he discovers quite how much he misses her. What's wrong with him? Is he finally turning into the man she always wanted him to be? And is this a good, or a bad thing?

'Leaves you believing not only in the redemptive power of music but above all the redemptive power of love. Funny and wise, sweet and true' *Independent*

PENGUIN ESSENTIALS

WHITE TEETH/ZADIE SMITH

'While he slipped in and out of consciousness, the position of the planets, the music of the spheres, the flap of a tiger-moth's diaphanous wings in Central Africa, and a whole bunch of other stuff that Makes Shit Happen had decided it was second-chance time for Archie . . .'

When fate steps in and roundly ruins divorced forty-seven-year-old Archie Jones' suicide attempt, he seizes his second life by the horns and promptly meets and marries Clara Bowden, a Caribbean girl twenty-eight years his junior. Thus begins a tale of friendship, love, war, three cultures and three families over three generations . . .

'A rollicking good read' *Independent*

A SHORT HISTORY OF TRACTORS IN UKRAINIAN/MARINA LEWYCKA

'Two years after my mother died, my father fell in love with a glamorous blonde Ukrainian divorcée. He was eighty-four and she was thirty-six . . .'

Voluptuous gold-digger Valentina loves green satin underwear, boil-in-the-bag cooking and, she insists, the émigré father of sisters Vera and Nadezhda. Putting aside a lifetime's feuding, the sisters will do anything to protect their father. Unfortunately for them, he doesn't want to be saved. Worse, the sisters' battle to keep their father from Valentina's clutches unearths troubling family secrets that reach back fifty years into Europe's dark history . . .

'Mad and hilarious' *Daily Telegraph*

PENGUIN ESSENTIALS

ANY HUMAN HEART/WILLIAM BOYD

'I have to start my real life soon, before I die of boredom and frustration . . .'

Logan Mountstuart – writer, lover, art dealer, spy – navigates his way through the twentieth century. In Paris he meets Hemingway and in London he argues with Virginia Woolf. Recruited as an agent by Ian Fleming, he is betrayed in the war and fetches up in sixties New York as artists begin to flock there. Throughout he seeks what each of us seeks – love, happiness and fulfilment – yet he makes the same mistakes we all do in finding it. Here, then, is a journey deep into a *very* human heart . . .

'Superb, wonderful, enjoyable' *Guardian*

TWILIGHT/ELIE WIESEL

'As a boy, Raphael feared madness but was drawn to madmen.'

A professor of literature and a Holocaust survivor, Raphael longs to find Pedro, the man who rescued him as an orphan in postwar Poland. But Pedro vanished inside the prisons of Stalin's Russia. When a mysterious caller directs him to the Mountain Clinic, an asylum for those whose delusions spring from the Bible, he finds patients calling themselves Adam, Cain, Abraham, Joseph, Jeremiah, and God. Searching for Pedro among them, Raphael seeks the meaning of his own survival . . .

'Wiesel has the literary talent and the moral ferocity to make our daily concerns seem trivial' *New York Times*

PENGUIN ESSENTIALS

A START IN LIFE/ANITA BROOKNER

'Dr Weiss, at forty, knew that her life had been ruined by literature.'

Beautiful, intelligent but lonely academic Ruth Weiss studies Balzac trying to work out exactly where her own life went wrong. Yet as she finds herself examining her childhood in London, the friendships that once meant so much to her and the ill-fated relationships she embarked on in Paris, she sees that her life has not been quite the series of missteps she had once thought. That perhaps there is still a chance at happiness, a new start . . .

'Enormously sophisticated, knowing, often very funny tragi-comedy'
Financial Times

THE ROAD TO LICHFIELD/PENELOPE LIVELY

'The tide's against us, hadn't you noticed? People haven't got that much time for the past nowadays'

Anne Linton is living a split life. Her father has suffered a stroke and most weekends she abandons her family and takes the road to Lichfield to be with him before he dies. But the longer she spends there, the more she is drawn into another life. Over a lingering summer she embarks on an affair, tries to save an old cottage from developers and discovers that her own father was not entirely the man she has always imagined him to be. As she begins to see the influence of the past everywhere she turns, Anne's present becomes more and more uncertain . . .

'Unfailingly literate, thoughtful and touching' *Washington Post*

PENGUIN ESSENTIALS

I'M THE KING OF THE CASTLE/SUSAN HILL

'Some people are coming here today, now you will have a companion.'

But young Edmund Hooper doesn't want anyone else in Warings, the large and rambling Victorian house he shares with his widowed father. Nevertheless Charles Kingshaw and his mother are soon installed and Hooper sets about subtly persecuting the fearful new arrival.

In the woods, Charles fights back but he knows that his rival will always win the affections of the adults – and that worse is still to come . . .

'Equalled for poignancy and horror only in Lord of the Flies' *Sunday Telegraph*

REGENERATION/PAT BARKER

'I just don't think our war aims – whatever they may be – and we don't know – justify this level of slaughter.'

The poets and soldiers Siegfried Sassoon and Wilfred Owen are dispatched to Craiglockhart War Hospital in Scotland in 1917. There, army psychiatrist William Rivers is treating brutalised, shell-shocked men. It is Rivers' job to fix these men and make them ready to fight again. As a witness to the traumas they have endured, can he in all conscience send them back to the horrors of the trenches?

'Brilliant, intense, subtle' *Sunday Times*

PENGUIN ESSENTIALS

THE DAY OF THE TRIFFIDS/JOHN WYNDHAM

'When a day that you happen to know is Wednesday starts off
by sounding like Sunday, there is something seriously wrong
somewhere.'

When a freak cosmic event renders most of the Earth's population blind,
Bill Masen – one of the lucky few to keep his sight – finds himself
trapped in a London jammed with sightless mobs who prey on those
who can still see. But another menace stalks blind and sighted alike.
With nobody to stop them the Triffids – walking carnivorous plants with
lethal stingers – rise up as humanity stumbles and falls . . .

'One of those books that haunts you for the rest of your life' *Sunday
Times*

THE MAN IN THE HIGH CASTLE/PHILIP K. DICK

'Truth, she thought. As terrible as death. But harder to find.'

America, fifteen years after the end of the Second World War. The
winning Axis powers have divided their spoils: the Nazis control New
York, while California is ruled by the Japanese. But between these
two states – locked in a cold war – lies a neutal buffer zone in which
legendary author Hawthorne Abendsen is rumoured to live. Abendsen
lives in fear of his life for he has written a book in which World War
Two was won by the Allies . . .

'The most brilliant sci-fi mind on any planet' *Rolling Stone*